Squint

Copyright © 2023 by Sherry Phinney

To Sue, Editor in Chief extraordinaire.

CHAPTER 1

"Damn, damn, damn!"

The headmaster paused on his way up the stairs to look for the source of the whisper. With the clouds and mist making it difficult to see, he accessed his search talent and discovered a child sitting in the bushes beneath one of the windows.

He quietly headed in that direction. As he neared the bushes, he heard scrambling, and the child appeared, clutching a small bag.

"I'm-sorry-I know-I'm-not-supposed-to-be-here-I'll leave right now," blurted the child all in one breath while turning to leave.

He touched the child on the shoulder and said, "No need to be in such a hurry. It's wet out here. Let's go inside where we can talk, shall we?"

The child appeared young, maybe seven or eight, with cropped reddish-brown hair, and nondescript clothing. Looking unhappy, the child shrugged and moved to his side.

As they turned towards the stairs, he said, "My name is Master McGillin. I'm the headmaster here. What's your name?"

"Squint, Sir."

"Squint?"

"Yes, Sir. My father said that when I was born, I was so small he had to squint to see me. He started calling me that as a joke, and it stuck. Now everybody calls me Squint."

Once they were settled in the headmaster's office, McGillin asked if Squint would like him to ring the head cook for some lunch.

For the first time showing real panic, Squint held up the small bag and said, "No, no, no. I have some lunch here. I'll be happy to share with you!"

"I'm sure the cook can –"

Squint quickly interrupted him and said, "Oh, no, sir. Please don't call the cook!"

With real interest, McGillin asked, "Is there a particular reason you don't want me to call the cook, Squint?"

Taking a deep breath, Squint said, "Yes, sir. My grammy is the head cook. She says I'm not supposed to be hanging around here, and if I get caught, she could get in trouble and lose her job. You're not going to make her leave just because of me, are you? It's my first time getting caught, so maybe you can give me another chance?"

Not "my first time," he noted, but "my first time getting caught". "Well, let's start with an explanation of what you were doing out there, shall we?"

Again, Squint took a deep breath before speaking, and in a rush, said. "Well, I was *trying* to learn about runes from Master Baxter, but he's not a very good teacher. Mr. Johnson says you can't buy books about runes, so he doesn't have any that I can borrow, so I have to rely on Master Baxter to help me understand how they work. But he's not as good as the other teachers at making you understand what they're teaching."

"The other teachers?"

"Yeah, like Mistress Roseman. She's really good at helping everyone understand what she's trying to say, and she pays attention to their questions and stuff. Master Baxter doesn't seem like he cares. He just stands in the front and reads from the book.

He doesn't even pay attention to whether or not the kids in the class understand what he's talking about."

"Who is Mr. Johnson," asked McGillin.

"He's the bookseller in town. When he has books he thinks I'll like, he lets me borrow them for free, as long as I'm careful with them. He's really nice, and he always has something new and interesting for me to read."

After a moment of thought, McGillin asked, "So how many of these classes have you listened in on?"

With some trepidation, Squint said, "If I tell you, it's not going to get Grammy in trouble, is it?"

"Absolutely not."

"Okay. Well, there are four windows on each side of this building, except the front. There are two on the north side of the front, and then the one I was at on the south side. The one I was at today is the last one with a class for me to listen to. So fifteen, in all. Well, I guess that's not exactly right. There were some that I started listening to that were about stuff I'd already learned from Mr. Johnson's books, so I skipped those. I think there were three of those. There were two classes that were languages I had already learned from books, so I only listened to those long enough to work out the pronunciation, which is hard to learn from books. And one of the windows on the north side of the front doesn't have a class. Guess that's this room. So nine, I guess, counting the runes class."

"How long have you been doing this, Squint," asked McGillin.

"About three years," said Squint, "More in dwowen and midden than in esan. It's so cold in esan, that the teachers mostly keep the windows shut. I miss things in dwowen a lot because of the rain, too. Midden is best, because it's nice all season. You're not going to tell Grammy I've been doing it that much, are you? She'll be upset, and I don't like to upset her."

"Let's see how things work out. How old are you, Squint?"

"I'm ten, Sir. I know I'm small for my age, but I'm smart," said Squint. "Mr. Johnson says that I learn faster than anyone he's ever known."

"It certainly appears that way," said McGillin. "Are you planning on attending the academy when you're old enough?"

"Oh, no, Sir." Squint paused and then said, "I have no talents, so I'm not eligible."

McGillin smiled at Squint and said, "I'll tell you what we'll do. Let's have your grandmother bring us some lunch, and the three of us will see if we can't work out a way for you to attend classes *inside* the building, since you're pretty much attending them anyway. What do you say to that?"

Squint ate in silence as Headmaster McGillin and her grandmother discussed her future.

She was trying to work through the current discussion, which seemed to be that Squint would continue to live with her grandmother while she attended classes, since her grandmother lived just outside the academy grounds. That seemed sensible, but they were discussing this as though Squint would be beginning classes immediately. She assumed she was misunderstanding something, because she knew that you had to be twelve to attend classes. She also knew that most students either had a special talent or multiple talents. She was a ten-year-old female, which meant no talents, so she wasn't sure how she would be allowed to attend at all, let alone immediately.

She did notice that her grandmother appeared to be avoiding any reference to Squint's gender. It wasn't clear whether she was doing so deliberately, but since the headmaster seemed to assume that Squint was male, and since girls were rarely allowed at the academy, it was fine with Squint.

As she was pondering this, she looked up to find both adults looking at her expectantly.

"So are you ready to see it?" asked her grandmother.

Having been lost in her own thoughts and paying little attention to what the adults had been discussing, and not knowing what else to do, she replied, "Sure," and gave them a huge smile.

The three walked through the hallway and around the corner to a massive set of double doors. They had been swung most of the way open, and what Squint saw within brought her to an abrupt halt. She squeaked out, "Is that real? Really real? It's not an illusion?"

Her grandmother gave her an indulgent smile, and Headmaster McGillin urged her forward with a nudge.

She entered the library with a look of utter awe on her face. "I didn't know there were this many books in the whole world," she said. "Where did they all come from? How did they get here? Why are they all here?"

The headmaster smiled at her and said, "Once we finish getting you enrolled in the academy, you will have complete access to the library. Usually, we don't allow books to be removed from the grounds, but I think we can make an occasional exception so that you can take a few of them home to read. Go ahead, wander around and get a feel for the place. Your grandmother and I will go finish getting you enrolled."

CHAPTER 2

After finishing breakfast, Serran Nylls, better known as Squint, asked her mother if she wanted help cleaning up. Her mother said, "No, that's okay. With your father just back from hunting, he can help me with the clean up. We'll need to spend the day skinning the animals and getting the meat ready to sell. Tomorrow you can help us get the skins ready for tanning. For today, why don't you take Jayden and go play at the beach. By Friday, we'll have everything finished and we'll be ready to celebrate your seventh birthday. We have some special surprises for you this year."

The Nylls family lived in the small village of Eslan, not far north of the town of Kenna. Her father was a hunter, and they sold the meat from whatever he killed for a living. In addition, her mother was an accomplished seamstress and turned the tanned hides into various items to sell in town. They made a good living, and their lives were comfortable and happy.

In addition to being a hunter, her father was a skilled carpenter, and the house they lived in was the best house in town. It was large, with three bedrooms, a fully stocked kitchen, and a separate sitting room. The house was beautifully built, and her mother had worked hard to create two wonderful gardens outside, one that provided the vegetables and herbs they needed, and a second just for flowers.

Squint took her four-year-old brother's hand, and the two of them set out for the beach.

The weather was great, and the two spent the whole morning playing on the beach. There were several other kids from the village there, and they all worked together to build the biggest sand castle ever.

They were almost done with the mote when Mr. Bronday, the mayor of the village, came by. He was a large, muscled, rather ugly man. He was mean and disliked everyone except his own wife and children. Although, as far as Squint could tell, he wasn't very nice to them, either.

He kicked the sand castle, and said, "What's this stupid thing supposed to be? Shouldn't you all be home helping your parents, or studying, or something? You make too much noise."

His house was not far from the beach, and he behaved like the beach was his own private beach. He kicked the castle again and told them to go home.

As the kids scattered, he said, "Squint, you tell your parents that I'll be by this afternoon to talk to them about the house."

Mr. Bronday had been pestering Squint's parents for several years to sell him their house. He felt that, as mayor, he should have the best of everything, including Squint's home. Her parents had spent years and a lot of hard work to get the house and grounds just as they wanted them, and were not willing to give it up, especially for the meager amount Mr. Bronday was offering to pay them.

Squint said, "Yes, Mr. Bronday, I'll be sure to tell them." She took Jayden's hand, and they hurried away from the beach. As they left, he shouted, "Make sure they know that I expect them to be there to talk to me this time."

When they got home, Squint told her parents about Mr. Bronday kicking down the sand castle. Then she delivered the message about him coming by this afternoon.

Her father said, "I wish that man would just get it through his thick head that we are not selling him our home. I don't know what else I can say that will convince him. Well, all I can do is tell him again. In the meantime, let's take a break and have some lunch, shall we?"

After a quick lunch of bread and cheese, Squint's father asked her if she would take Jayden back to the beach for the afternoon.

"Aw, Dad, I have that new book that I got from Mr. Johnson. Can't I stay here and read that? I'll keep an eye on Jayden while I read."

"Take the book to the beach with you. It'll be easier for us to get things accomplished if you two aren't under foot," he replied.

"What if I get it wet, or get sand on it or something. I don't want to spoil one of Mr. Johnson's books. He won't let me borrow any more if I ruin a book," said Squint.

"I know you well enough to know you'll be extremely careful not to damage his book, Squint," said her mother. "You two go on and have a good time at the beach. At least you know Mr. Bronday won't show up," she said.

"Okay, I get the message." Squint asked Jayden if he was ready to go back to the beach. He plopped down on his butt, and said, "Nope, not going. Nope. Nope. Staying here with Daddy. Yup. Staying here with Daddy."

Squint sighed. "Come on Jayden, Mom and Dad need to get things done today, and they don't need us in the way," she said.

"I don't care. I'm not going. I'm staying here. I'll be as quiet as a mouse. Daddy, can't I stay here with you?"

"All right," said Squint's mother. "Squint, you go ahead and go to the beach. I'm sure Jayden will end up taking a nap anyway."

"Well, if he's going to nap, can't I stay in my room and read?"

"Squint, please, I don't have time to argue with you. You'll have a good time at the beach," said her mother.

Admitting defeat, Squint retrieved Mr. Johnson's book on botany and headed for the beach. She spent the next several hours reading.

Suddenly, Squint's head shot up. Something was wrong! Something terrible was happening at home!

She grabbed her book and ran as fast as she could for the house. As she approached, she realized she might not want to rush right in without knowing what was going on. So she slowed to a walk and quietly approached the living room window.

As she neared the window, she heard a loud crash, and heard her mother shout, "No!" She heard another crash, and then another. She could hear noises inside, and she heard someone mumbling. Very frightened now, she slowly crept closer to the house, and crouched down behind the bushes underneath the window.

This close, the mumbling was loud enough that she was able to make out words. She recognized the voice as Mr. Bronday's. "Stupid idiots. They should have just sold me the damn house. All right, I need to get these bodies out of here and get this mess cleaned up. And I need to get rid of the other brat. I'll just tell everyone that they sold me the house and left the village. They should have just sold me the house. This should be *my* house. I'm the mayor. No one should have a better house than mine. Stupid idiots."

Clutching her book, Squint remained quietly hidden in the bushes under the window while Mr. Bronday removed the bodies of her family. Although he was gone for some time, she was too afraid to move. He finally returned to clean up the mess in the house. When he left, he was still muttering to himself about how stupid her parents were. She waited until she was sure he would not be returning, and went into the house. Dazed, she sat down at the kitchen table and cried.

After a time, she realized that she needed to get out of there, before Mr. Bronday came looking for her to finish what he started. As she went through the house, she discovered three packages hidden in her mother's closet. Birthday presents from her family.

She set the packages, along with Mr. Johnson's book, on the porch, and went back inside.

She picked up the lantern from the fireplace mantle and spread the oil over the floor. She did the same with all the other lanterns in the house. Once finished, she went outside, picked up her birthday gifts and the book, and dropped a match inside the door. She turned and left, and headed for her grandmother's house in nearby Kenna.

As she reached the top of the hill outside of the village, she turned, and noticed that the house wasn't burning. Her anger rose, and something in her flared out. She watched as flames rose up and consumed the house she was born in. Mr. Bronday would *not* be living in the Nylls home.

CHAPTER 3

After six weeks at the academy, Squint was finally settling in to the daily routine. Squint and her grandmother began their days by eating breakfast and then walking to the campus together.

The campus was made up of seven buildings. On the western side of the campus, , there were two dormitory buildings at the north, and the building holding the level two classrooms to the south. In the center of the campus, the northern-most building held the kitchen and cafeteria, while the administration building--which housed the staff offices, library, and level one classrooms--was to the south. On the eastern side, there was a huge three-story building that housed the gymnasium, theater and the magic training center at the northern end, with a smaller building that held the level three classrooms at the south.

Shortly after beginning classes, Squint realized that, because of the layout of the campus and the location of her grandmother's home to the northeast between the campus and Kenna, her wanderings had only brought her to the level one classes. She hadn't wandered far enough to find the two buildings with the more challenging level two and level three classrooms.

During their morning walk to campus, Squint's grandmother, Cayrah Nylls, reached her destination first. At that point, Squint, not being one of the more popular students, normally finished the walk to the level two building by herself.

Since she was not old enough to officially attend the academy, Headmaster McGillin had arranged for Squint to "sit in" on several classes. She did the lessons and took the tests, just as the other students did. However, her scores were not official and were not entered into any academy records. This was not supposed to be general knowledge, but of course everyone knew.

This was fine with Squint, since her goal was learning, and not scoring high on tests. For some of the boys, however, the competition to get the best scores was fierce and would sometimes verge on violence. These boys seemed to resent the fact that Squint's scores went unrecorded, especially since her scores were frequently the highest in the class. Also, because Squint didn't live on campus, she didn't participate in any of the boys' evening activities. This, paired with her unofficial classroom status, made Squint an outsider among the students.

One of the upper level students, Quellan Greves, seemed to have formed a particular animosity toward her. He would go out of his way to find her and torment her any time he thought he could do so without getting caught. And he was very good at judging when and where he could get away with his creative torments. Squint did her best to avoid these confrontations. Since studying was definitely not one of Quellan's favorite activities, Squint spent as much of her spare time as possible in the library. Here, Squint could avoid any aggrieved students and get on with her studies. Besides, as far as Squint was concerned, the library was the most amazing place in the world.

Squint was still amazed at the size of the library and the number and variety of books it contained. Since beginning classes at the academy, Squint had learned that this campus was only one of many campuses world-wide that made up The Academies for the Talented. Not only that, it was one of the smallest of the campuses, and had one of the smallest libraries. To her, this was absolutely amazing, and she hoped that one day she might be able to visit some of the larger libraries.

Squint had some secrets that she was keeping. Spending her time in the library with minimal interaction with staff and other students, made it easier to keep her secrets safe.

The first secret, of course, was the fact that she was female. Since the main objective of the academy was to teach students to master their talents, and since females did not have talents, she didn't think she would be able to continue classes at the academy if it became known that she was female. Although there had been a few rare instances where females had been allowed at the academy to be taught and groomed as teachers, she wasn't sure she would qualify. So she took care to do nothing that would reveal her gender. At her current age, and because she lived off campus, this was fairly simple. But she was smart enough to know that as she grew older, it would become more difficult.

The second secret was much bigger and much more difficult to conceal. This was a secret that was hers alone. Before her parents died, her mother had been aware of the secret, but her father and grandmother had never known. This secret had apparently frightened her mother, and so Squint had been taught from a very early age to keep it hidden. Although she was unclear about the reason for her mother's fear, she had always been careful to abide by her mother's wishes in the matter. When her parents died and she moved in with her grandmother, she continued to keep this secret.

Until Squint was able to do some research on the subject and get more information, she was unwilling to reveal this secret to anyone. She would just have to continue to work hard to keep it hidden.

As Squint entered the library, she was greeted by Master Teslan, the head librarian. "Good morning, Squint. No class this morning?"

"The history master is ill, so class was canceled," she replied.

"So you have some extra time. Good, I want to show you something. Come with me."

She was a bit annoyed, since she wanted to find the next book in the series of mathematical physics she had been studying. Still, she obediently stepped to his side. Maybe he would have something new and interesting to show her.

As he led her into the western portion of the library, he said, "I've noticed that you have never read anything from the fiction section, and I wanted to introduce you to some of the opportunities you're missing out on."

Disappointed, she said, "I've read fiction. Once, after I read a Tayran dictionary, I asked Mr. Johnson if I could borrow some books in the Tayran language. The only books he had were some fiction books he bought for Mrs. Elya. I read them so I could understand the language, but they were silly."

"Mrs. Elya, the widow from town? Yes, I've met her, and my guess is what you were reading were romances," he said. "I can certainly understand why you would find those silly. But the books I'm talking about are very different from those. Let me choose a book or two for you, and we'll see what you think. I'll even let you take a few home with you to read in the evening."

They wandered among the shelves, and Master Teslan chose four books from among the vast array available. "These should do for a start. I am giving these books to you as an assignment, and I expect you to read all of them from beginning to end. You've been given a mystery, an adventure, a fantasy and a comedy. When you've finished them, I expect a verbal report on which of the genres you enjoyed most, and why."

"I'm betting that you will actually enjoy reading one or two of them. At the very least, these books will teach you that there are more ways to learn than studying textbooks."

She very much liked and respected Master Teslan, so she would do as he asked, even though she was not particularly happy about this assignment. Her only consolation was that she could take the books home with her, so she wouldn't be wasting her time at the library on them. Looking at the size of the books, she could probably finish them in an evening or two and be done with it.

As she tucked the books under her arm and they headed back to the front desk, they heard a loud voice say, "Hey, where is everybody? I'm here and nobody's here to greet me." They recognized the voice as belonging to Young Donald, the First Librarian's Assistant.

Young Donald—Young, because his grandfather was Old Donald—was a tall rangy redhead, with one of the most mellow personalities Squint had ever encountered. He was perpetually happy and nothing seemed to upset him. He was also one of the laziest people she had ever met. His talent was an ability to convince people that whatever he was saying was the absolute truth, so he rarely had to do things for himself. There was always someone around that he could convince to do things for him. Fortunately, he was also incredibly sweet, and never got carried away with his requests.

"And what were the two of you doing back there all alone in the dark stacks," he smirked.

Squint wrinkled her nose and nodded at her stack of books. "Picking fiction for me to read," she said.

He glanced from Squint to Master Teslan, grinned hugely, and said, "Hmmm, picking fiction. That's a new one, but I guess I can pretend I believe it."

It was clear that Squint missed the innuendo, but Master Teslan did not. "That's enough Young Donald. You're late, and you have a lot to do. You still haven't finished the upkeep on the books in the restricted area."

"Restricted area," thought Squint. "Now that sounds intriguing. Much more interesting than the fiction section."

"Oh, all right. Can I take Squint with me? I can probably find something for him to do," said Young Donald.

"No. This time you'll have to do the work yourself," said the librarian. "Squint has his own assignment. And besides, isn't it time for you to be heading for your next class, Squint?"

Squint said, "Oh, yes. I'll be late if I don't hurry," and headed for the door. "Thank you for the books Master Teslan."

As she hurried down the stairs at the front of the administration building, Squint was paying no attention to her surroundings. She was thinking about the restricted area of the library, wondering how she could get access and what she might find there.

Suddenly, she felt a shove in the middle of her back. She went rolling down the remainder of the stairs, and the books that Master Teslan had chosen for her went flying.

She landed hard, flat on her back, at the bottom of the stairs. As she lay there trying to catch her breath and assess the damage, she looked up to see Quellan Greves standing beside her with a nasty grin on his face.

"Oh dear," he said. "How clumsy you are. You seem to have fallen down the stairs. Here, let me help you up."

She ignored the hand he extended and scrambled to her feet. Winded and breathing hard, she looked around, trying to find her books. But Quellan apparently wasn't done with her. He elbowed her in the shoulder and sent her flying again. This time, she landed hard on her butt.

"Oh, my, now I'm the clumsy one," he said. He looked around and gathered up her books. "Let's see what Mister Studious has this time."

"Fiction? Since when do you read fiction?" He viciously tossed the books into the bushes next to the building, and turned to Squint with a look on his face that said she was in for something very unpleasant. As she always did when she was upset, she touched the stone her mother had given her.

Having been on the receiving end of Quellan's animosity more than once, Squint feared she was not going to get off lightly this time. As much as she hated doing so, she was going to have to do something to prevent Quellan doing serious damage. She lightly touched one of her talents. She "pushed" Master Teslan and suggested that he needed a breath of fresh air. She added a sense of urgency to the push, and hoped that he would react quickly.

As far as Squint knew, she was the only female who possessed a talent. Boys had talents; girls did not. That's just the way it was. Most boys had a single talent, some had two, and rarely, a boy would have three talents. But girls did not have talents. Period.

Except Squint did have a talent—and not just one. She had many talents. A great many. Keeping these talents under control and hidden was becoming more difficult every day. Especially from people like Headmaster McGillin, who was very deft at using his search and audio talents to keep track of what was happening on campus.

Consequently, Squint used her talents sparingly, and only when she was reasonably sure that no one was near enough to sense what she was doing. But right now, she needed something to happen quickly, or she could end up seriously hurt.

In moments, Master Teslan appeared at the top of the steps, looking around in mild confusion, as if unsure what he was doing there. He found Squint sitting on the ground at the foot of the stairs, with Quellan leaning over her, hand raised threateningly.

"Quellan, what on earth do you think you're doing! Move away from him immediately," shouted Master Teslan as he quickly headed down the stairs.

Quellan, red-faced with anger, stepped away from Squint and glared at the librarian. "He was asking for it," he snapped. "Little brat thinks he's better than the rest of us, always kissing up to the teachers and showing off how smart he is. Even you think he can do no wrong. Look at you, automatically assuming this is all my fault, without even bothering to find out what's going on."

"Quellan," replied Master Teslan sternly, "you are nearly six years Squint's senior and twice his size. Nothing he could have done to you would warrant what you were about to do. Besides, I know for a fact that he was in a hurry to get to class, and would not have stopped just to aggravate you."

Which, of course, just fueled Quellan's anger. Without another word, he turned and stomped off. Squint was pretty sure there would be hell to pay later.

Master Teslan bent over and helped Squint stand up. "Are you all right, Squint?" he asked.

"I'm fine," Squint replied. "I need to find my books," she said.

"Let me help," said Master Teslan.

As they searched the bushes for the books, Master Teslan asked if she had this kind of problem often.

"Most of the boys dislike me. They think that I'm getting special treatment, and they don't like it. And they think I'm showing off when I get stuff right in class. I try to keep it to myself, but the teachers keep asking me things, and I just can't pretend I don't know the answers," she said. "Quellan's the only one that gets really mean about it, though."

They found the last book, and Master Teslan offered to walk with her to class to explain why she was late.

"Oh, no," she exclaimed. "I don't need to give anyone any more reason to dislike me. But thank you, all the same."

CHAPTER 4

While she waited for her grandmother to finish getting ready for their weekly trip to the bazaar in town, Squint sat in her room, fingering the last gift from her mother and thinking.

The latest book in a series of mysteries sat open on her lap, although she wasn't currently reading. Since her first "fiction assignment" from Master Teslan, she had continued to choose fiction books to take home to read. Not only did it mean she got to read at home, but she actually found them entertaining.

The necklace she was handling was one of the three gifts she had rescued from her mother's closet before leaving Eslan.

One gift had been a book on botanical medicine from her father, with a note suggesting that she not read it all at once. As a way to honor him, she had read it slowly, one chapter at a time. She now kept it on the nightstand by her bed, and sometimes re-read it the same way, one chapter at a time, to once again honor her father.

The second gift had been a piece of misshapen clay, with a note from her brother (in her mother's handwriting) wishing her a happy birthday, and saying he made her a puppy to be her friend. It did vaguely resemble something with a head and tail, and she kept that on her nightstand, too. It sometimes made her cry to look at it, but mostly it made her happy to think of Jayden, sitting at the kitchen table and concentrating on making this gift for her.

The third gift had been from her mother. It was a small stone, beautifully set in silver filigree, hung on a slender silver chain. The stone itself was more or less oval in shape, about the size of a large grape. It was translucent, with tiny streaks of color that changed with the light. It had come with a note that said that this was a special gift, and her mother would explain later. Of course, there had been no later for her mother, so the explanation had never come. This gift Squint always wore around her neck.

The stone's translucency and colors seemed to change with Squint's mood. Squint was sure there was something truly special about the stone. When she was upset or frightened, she would finger the stone through the cloth of her shirt, and it seemed to calm her. It also seemed to help her focus when she was using her talents.

Whenever she got a chance, she would search the library for information about the stone. Although she had found nothing relating to the stone, she *had* come across some information that she thought might explain her possession of talents.

She was thinking that being less than popular and living off campus helped keep her talents secret, but she needed to find a place where she could experiment with her ever-growing list of abilities. As she neared her twelfth birthday, she was discovering more talents, and finding it more difficult to identify and control them.

She needed somewhere she could practice using the various talents to find out what she was capable of doing with them. She needed to work out how she could combine different talents for different results, and how to control the results. She had found a way to mask her use of talents, but so far, when she experimented with the ability, she found that it left a void that was even more obvious than the talent it was masking.

And it's not like there was anyone she could ask. There was the library, but the information available in the main sections regarding talents was very limited. There is no need for information on combining talents, since no one person had enough talents to need to learn how to combine them. And talents, by themselves, were pretty straightforward.

It would be perfect if she could make use of the magic training center, where there were protections in place to prevent "accidents," but that was out of the question. She had considered using the woods to the east of Kenna, but she was afraid she would set them on fire, or something worse. She did need to find something soon, before she made a mistake and someone discovered her secret.

Squint had been allowed to accompany Young Donald on a few of his trips to the restricted area of the library. The area was in the center of the library, was enclosed in glass, and was kept locked at all times. The materials in this area were here for one of two reasons; either they contained "forbidden" information, or the books themselves were rare and needed special care of some sort.

There weren't many books of the forbidden sort. Most of these books included information on creating runes and mystic symbols for use with magical talents. These were restricted because they were easily misused, either intentionally or accidently, so their use was strictly monitored.

In glancing through some of the rare books, she had found a small one called *The Sacrifice of the Talents*, by Mistress Warren. This was the book she suspected contained information relevant to her possession of talents. She hadn't had time to read much, but what she had found was a bit frightening. She needed more time with the book, preferably alone, to find out what it could tell her.

And now, there were rumors going around that girls were being born with talents. And that they were being born with at least three or four talents, not just one. This fit in with what she had been able to read in the restricted book. She *needed* to get back to that book.

"You ready, Serran?" asked her grandmother, as she poked her head around the door. "Let's go see what trouble we can get into, shall we?"

Saturday was Squint's favorite day of the week. It was her grandmother's only day off from cafeteria duties, and she and her grandmother spent the day together doing the weekly shopping at the bazaar in Kenna, eating at one of the many restaurants available, and visiting with friends.

Today, they took their time choosing the perfect piece of fish, and the "just right" fruit, discussing the past week's events, while they slowly made their way through the bazaar. They decided to choose some fruit and cheese to eat at the park, rather than eating at a restaurant, since it was such a lovely day.

After lunch, Squint left her grandmother sitting in the park with friends, and headed for Mr. Johnson's book shop. Although she had no need to borrow books from him any more, she still enjoyed visiting with him. Since making fiction part of her life, she found that Mr. Johnson also enjoyed fiction, and the two of them shared similar tastes. They often arranged to read the same book, and would discuss it the next time Squint visited.

As she wandered through town on her way to the bookstore, she heard a familiar, nasty voice behind her. In utter fear, she turned around to see Mr. Bronday, from the village of Eslan, shouting at some unfortunate person who seemed to have offended him. Apparently, he didn't come to Kenna often, because she had not seen him since the day her family died. If he saw her, would he come after her? She didn't want to find out, but there was nowhere to go. Terrified, she fingered her birthday stone, and wished she was somewhere else, preferably at home, where it was safe and he couldn't find her.

Squint looked around her room in confusion. What just happened? How on earth did she come to be in her room?

Another new talent. It had to be. Nothing else made sense. Somehow, in her fear, she must have triggered a talent that allowed her to travel instantly. This was not a talent she had heard of before, but she was discovering she had a lot of those. She assumed there were a lot of talents she hadn't heard about yet.

She could add this to her growing list of talents to be explored, but for now, she had to get back to her grandmother without attracting the attention of Mr. Bronday. She sat for a moment, wondering if she dared use one of her newest talents when she got back to Kenna.

She had recently discovered that she was able to blur the air around her in such a way that others were unable to see her. For her, it left a void where it was obvious something *should* be, but apparently others didn't see this. This talent was new enough that she hadn't had a chance to test it, so there were things about it that she was still unsure of. Could she move while she was using it? Did people have talents that would allow them to see through it? Talents that would sense the same void she did?

Even being unsure of all of that, it should be sufficient to prevent Mr. Bronday, who wasn't very observant, from seeing her if she should encounter him again.

She decided to continue her day as if it had not been interrupted, and successfully reached the bookstore without encountering Mr. Bronday again. After an enjoyable visit discussing fiction with Mr. Johnson, she headed back to the park to meet her grandmother.

As she made her way through town, she realized that it would be wise to broaden the area of her scrutiny when she was searching for trouble. She frequently did a "sweep" of the campus to check on Quellan Greves' location, so she could avoid confrontations with him. She would need to start doing them wherever she was, so she could avoid chance encounters with Mr. Bronday as well.

Once she got to the park, she found a place near her grandmother where she would not be easily seen, and settled in. Although she had a book in her lap, she was not reading. While she watched her grandmother enjoying herself with friends, she thought about the implications of this newest talent. If she could get control of this talent and learn to travel at will, she could use it to gain access to the magic center to practice her other talents.

She knew that, while the gymnasium was left open so the boys had access in the evenings, the two upper floors, which held the theater and magic center, were kept locked. For obvious reasons, there were no windows in the magic center, so she would be able to practice without being seen, and without worrying about any damage she might cause.

She would be able to travel to the magic center in the evenings, when the room would be unoccupied. This would, however, require hiding her absence from her grandmother, and she wasn't sure she could, or even wanted, to do this.

She was discovering new talents at an alarming rate, and she desperately needed a way to learn to control and use them.

She also had another problem that would need to be dealt with soon. When she reached her twelfth birthday, she would be old enough to be officially enrolled in the academy. This would require filling out paperwork which would include her real name, making it clear that she was female. She did not want to lose her position at the academy. Perhaps, if neither she nor her grandmother mentioned her birthday, no one would remember to change her status.

And then there was the *big* problem. She was smart enough, even without talents, to know that it wasn't going to be long before it started to become obvious that she was a female. The changes were already starting. She was either going to have to come clean about being female, which would probably mean leaving the academy, or she was going to have to explore ways to hide the physical changes.

It was time to let her grandmother in on her secret. Squint had always disliked keeping her secret from her grandmother, but now it was necessary to share. She was going to need her grandmother's help to keep her secret safe while she learned.

Besides, she wanted someone to talk to when she had concerns, and she wanted to be able to concentrate on her talents without fear of discovery while she was at home. It was, for now, the only safe place to practice.

The following evening, when they sat down for dinner, Squint said, "Gramma, there's something we need to talk about."

Her grandmother looked at her and said, "Something happened in town yesterday, didn't it?"

Unsure exactly how to start, Squint said, "I saw Mr. Bronday. It scared me and made something happen that we really need to talk about." She took a deep breath and blurted, "I have talents," and waited for her grandmother's response.

Her grandmother just sat and looked at her. "Is there more?" she finally asked.

"You don't seem surprised," said Squint.

"I've always known there was something special about you, Serran. Since you came to live with me, I've realized it was something remarkable. Now I know what it is. But you said "talents". You have more than one?"

Amazed at her grandmother's instant acceptance, and grateful that it was going to be so much easier than expected, Squint spent the rest of the evening discussing her talents with her grandmother.

Beginning with her rage at Mr. Bronday's murder of her family that triggered the use of the talent that destroyed her home, they discussed many things relating to Squint's possession of talents. They also discussed Squint's concerns about her future at the academy and her issues with Quellan Greves.

It was as if a huge weight had been lifted off Squint's shoulders. Sharing her fears and concerns with her grandmother made Squint realize just how much of a burden keeping secrets from her grandmother had been, and just how much she had needed someone to share her worries.

CHAPTER 5

For the first time in her life, the majority of Squint's time was spent on something other than her studies. She was spending far more time exploring her talents than on her studies. She actually found it amusing that her studies were taking a back seat to the talents that she was perfecting so that she could ensure her ability to continue with her studies.

With her grandmother now sharing the secret, she could openly work on her talents at home. She and her grandmother often discussed her various abilities, how best to make use of them, and ways to improve them. They also discussed the need to continue to hide her true gender, and the best way to accomplish that.

She was focusing on manipulating the talent that she had been using to make herself undetectable in such a way that she would be able to alter her appearance. She would need to sustain the illusion for long periods, and maintain it while she concentrated on other things. And she would need to find a way to remove the "void" it caused where she should appear, so that others wouldn't be able to penetrate the illusion.

She was getting better, but it wasn't perfect yet. Since it wasn't crucial at this point, she would continue to practice at home, but would put off using it anywhere else until she was sure it was perfected.

She was also working on her traveling talent. Once she mastered that, she could travel to the magic center to practice other talents. She would be able to spend some time in the evenings, when the center was unavailable to others, practicing safely.

Any time she found herself completely alone, she "hopped" a short distance. Since her first "trip" had been triggered by fear, it took her a while to figure out how to trigger the talent at will. She found that she just needed to picture where she wanted to go, and she could "think" herself to that place.

Because she wasn't sure what could happen if her image of the desired location wasn't accurate, she had only been traveling to places that were close enough to see from where she was. But that was accomplishing nothing. She needed to get over her fear and make real use of this talent. Today, she decided she was familiar enough with her bedroom to try a trip there.

She had no classes this afternoon, so she went to the kitchen, where her grandmother was working on the evening meal. It was late enough that most of the other staff would have already gone home She would wait until the last one left, and then attempt to travel to her bedroom and back to the kitchen.

If she succeeded, she would wait until after bedtime and try a trip to the restricted area of the library to finish reading *The Sacrifice of the Talents*. She hadn't told her grandmother about the book yet. She wanted to wait and see if it had anything useful first. Besides, she was pretty sure her grandmother wouldn't approve of her sneaking into the library.

Success! One minute she was standing beside her grandmother in the kitchen, the next in her bedroom. In excitement, she traveled back, grabbed her grandmother, and danced all around the kitchen.

Once they got over the initial excitement, she asked her grandmother if she would be willing to help Squint with an experiment. She wanted to see if she could take someone with her when she traveled. If she could manage that, her grandmother could come with her when she practiced in the magic center.

Her grandmother considered this while she finished her day's work in the kitchen. When she finished the last of her chores, she looked at Squint and said, "Well, you seem to be all in one piece. And it would be nice if I could go places with you. Maybe we could even take a vacation some time." She grinned and said, "Let's do it!"

Squint took her grandmother's hand and pictured both of them standing in the living room of their home. She took a deep breath and willed them home. Success again! Squint turned to her grandmother, who had a huge grin on her face.

"This is really strange," she said. "I didn't feel a thing. I'm just suddenly home, instead of at work. What a lazy way to get home at the end of the day. I could get used to this, Serran."

Squint and her grandmother spent the rest of the evening discussing the advantages and possible consequences of traveling this way. They talked about the best way to make use of the magic center, and whether there might be other uses for this talent.

At the end of the day, Squint lay in bed, waiting until she was sure her grandmother was asleep before traveling to the library. She was hoping *The Sacrifice of the Talents* would prove to have the answers she was looking for.

When she arrived--right where she intended--in the center of the restricted section of the library, she was surprised to hear someone humming. She immediately "blurred" herself and sat down beside the table of books in front of her so she couldn't be seen through the glass. She remained as still as she could while she tried to figure out who was in the library at this late hour.

It didn't take her long to recognize Master Teslan's voice. She sat very still for a time, waiting for him to leave, fingering her birthday stone to calm herself. It sounded like he was in the back of the fiction section, and it didn't sound like he was planning on leaving any time soon.

Since he was nowhere near where she was, she finally decided to risk getting the book and finding a safe place to read it. As long as she stayed blurred and was very quiet, it should be all right. He would have to unlock the door to the restricted area to discover her, and that would give her enough warning to travel out of the library before he noticed her.

By the time she finished *The Sacrifice of the Talents*, Master Teslan had left the library. He had absent-mindedly left the lights on, which suited Squint just fine. She needed to do some research, to establish the book's validity.

When she finally returned to her room, Squint sat on her bed for a long time, trying to decide if she should wake her grandmother. The research she had done had convinced her that the information in *The Sacrifice of the Talents* was valid, and this terrified her.

She reasoned that it was Friday—well Saturday, now—and they had nothing planned for the day. Waking her grandmother should be all right. They could sleep all day, if they wanted, although she was pretty sure they wouldn't. Besides, she really needed to share what she had learned.

Squint woke her grandmother, and asked her to join her at the kitchen table. This is where they sat whenever they had something serious to discuss, usually with a cup of hot tea or cocoa.

Without question, her grandmother went to the kitchen and started the kettle for tea. She looked at Squint and said, "I take it we're going to need this?"

Once settled at the table, Squint began by explaining to her grandmother how she had first come across *The Sacrifice of the Talents*, and the concerns it had caused. She then told her grandmother about traveling to the library, finishing the book, and the efforts she had taken to validate the information that it contained.

She asked for another cup of tea, and tried to assemble her thoughts while her grandmother heated another kettle of water. And then she shared what she had read.

The book stated that a bit over a millennium ago, there was a widely-respected prophet named Mella. Mella was known throughout the world for the accuracy of her predictions. In the course of her lifetime, she had made many predictions, and each had come to pass. Near the end of her life, Mella had made a prediction that would affect the entire world.

Mella had predicted that there would come a time, one thousand years from now, when a man would be born with untold powers, who would hold an unsurpassed hatred for humanity. He would be a magician with the ability and the desire to hold the world in a reign of terror, before causing its utter destruction.

If things were left to the fates, he would succeed.

But if humans were willing to make the sacrifice, they could provide the means to stop this magician's destruction of the world. And make no mistake, it would be a sacrifice. All humans would have to give up their talents, beginning now and continuing until the need to contain the power of the Magician arrived.

At the appropriate time, there would be born a child who would become the receptacle for all of the sacrificed talents. With the appropriate training, this human Receptacle would have enough power to prevent the Magician's destruction of the world. Once the Receptacle became aware of the possession of these talents, the sacrifice of talents would no longer be necessary, and talents would become available to all once again. This would be the sign that the time of the Magician had come.

The initial sacrifice of talents would have to be deliberate. Future sacrifices would be made involuntarily; babies would simply be born without talents.

The world's leaders met to discuss this prediction. They spent months discussing the probable accuracy of Mella's prediction, and if the suggested precaution was the best way to achieve the desired goal. Considering the accuracy of Mella's past predictions, it was finally decided that the risk of world destruction was not worth taking. The next step was to find the best way to make it happen.

There were several among the world leaders who had the ability to transfer talents to inanimate objects. This talent had been used on a few occasions, where there was a need to remove talents from people who were using them for criminal purposes. These leaders could transfer the talents to some kind of vessel.

This would affectively remove all existing talents. The vessel could be made to gather talents from all new-born babes,. It would hold all sacrificed talents until the appropriate time arrived. When the time of the Magician arrived, the talents would seek an appropriate Receptacle.

They had a master potter create a large, ostentatious vase, which would be the physical receptacle for the talents.

In working out the method for removing talents, the leaders had discovered that, if all of the leaders with the transfer talent worked together, they could transfer the talents of everyone in a large area at once, even if they were unseen. So the leaders traveled the world with their receptacle, collecting talents, until all talents had been transferred to the receptacle.

It was later discovered that there were some men among the leaders that decided they should not be included in the sacrifice. They were men and leaders; they should be allowed to keep a talent or two. These few men chose to retain one or two of their talents. For some unknown reason, this selfishness made it possible for future men to be born with talents.

By the time she finished sharing what she had read, it was light out, and they decided to have breakfast while they discussed the implications of the prophesy.

Squint said that, as far as she could tell, it was right about the time that she realized she had talents that other females with talents started appearing. And her own list of talents appeared to be endless. She had talents she had never heard of before, and was sure that there were many that she had yet to discover.

Squint's grandmother said that she remembered a big hullabaloo about a year after Squint was born regarding some vase that disappeared from the International Institute of Art in Melsta. Since it didn't have anything to do with her, she hadn't paid much attention.

They discussed the possibility that the stolen vase was the talent receptacle, and the likelihood that the thief was the Magician, who took the vase in an attempt to prevent its purpose being fulfilled.

"Maybe he thought that he could prevent the distribution of the talents if he destroyed the vase," Squint said. "But no matter what his reason for taking the vase was," she continued, "it means he's out there, is aware of the prophecy, and has mastered his talents well enough to have successfully stolen the vase from the high-security International Institute of Art. It also means he's much older than I am," Squint said.

"I have no idea why you were chosen to receive these talents, Serran," said her grandmother, "but you're going to have to keep vigilant. Until recently, he may have believed that he prevented the prophecy's fulfillment, but with females being born with talents, he will be aware that he failed. You can bet that he is searching for you, and will make every effort to destroy you when he finds you."

Squint reached over and gave her grandmother's hand a squeeze. "Yes, but I have one big advantage," she said. "He will be looking for a young girl with many talents, and you and I are the only people that know I'm a girl with talents. Everyone else thinks I'm a boy with no talents. I'm going to have to work to make sure it stays that way. I'll need to perfect the blurring talent, and work on other ways to hide my talents. And you're going to have to start calling me Squint," she said with a grin.

Squint and her grandmother recognized the need for Squint to work on discovering and mastering as many talents as possible, as quickly as possible.

After some discussion on what would work best, they decided that any talent with no danger involved, like her appearance illusion, could be practiced at home. Anything that might be dangerous in any way would be practiced at the magic center. Since the magic center was arranged with protective barriers for spectators, they could travel there three or four times a week, late in the evening, and her grandmother could safely watch while Squint experimented with her more dangerous talents.

This process worked very well, and Squint began learning and mastering new talents very quickly. She found that listening to other students discuss their successes and failures, and how they handled the failures, also provided inspiration for new things to try.

For the time being, she was omitting the high magics, those that involved runes and rituals, from her studies. While she eventually wanted to include them, right now, focusing on understanding her talents and how she could use and combine them was enough. Besides, any information she could access on the high magics was locked up in the library's restricted area. She didn't want to waste time sneaking in to the library at night.

At the magic center, she was experimenting with making use of the properties of the four elements, so she was working on different methods of producing and controlling various aspects of earth, fire, wind and water.

She was also working on her strength and accuracy throwing items at various targets. This included the elemental properties, but also included calling items to hand.

At home, after a few mishaps with vases and furniture, Squint learned to move objects to and from specific places, instantly and with accuracy. To practice, her grandmother would hide various items around the house. She would then name an item and state where she wanted it. Squint would first be required to ascertain its current location, and then put it where her grandmother had requested. From the beginning, ascertaining the location and moving it was easy. Placing it with accuracy was not nearly as easy. But she eventually got it right, and she could do it almost instantly and with amazing accuracy.

She often practiced altering her appearance or turning invisible in front of her bedroom mirror. When she altered her appearance, there was a slight blur that showed anywhere she made something appear different. So, if she made her long hair appear short, there was a blur in place of the hair she was hiding. It was very slight, but she needed to find a way to get rid of it.

She soon mastered the ability, and began making a slight alteration to her appearance that she maintained constantly, even at home. She wanted this ability to become second nature so she could maintain the altered appearance without thinking about it. She would change her looks as little as possible--just enough to make her appear male—which would help keep the effort of maintaining the illusion to a minimum.

She also continued working on getting rid of the void that was created when she attempted to "cloak" herself in invisibility.

She continued to work on perfecting her ability to monitor her surroundings with as little effort as possible. In the process of working on this talent, she had discovered that there were students who had the talent to "push" people, much like the one she had used to push Master Teslan to come to her aid against Quellan Greves shortly after she arrived.

As she had discovered in working with her own talent, this talent could be used to suggest a specific emotion, as well as an action.

So a person could "suggest" that you like them, or that you believe what they were saying. Or even that you dislike someone else. She met several students who used this talent who seemed to be totally unaware that they were doing so.

There were also students who, although they weren't able to push a person, could "probe" to see what you were thinking or feeling. Other than allowing someone to change their behavior to suit your mood, there didn't seem to be any practical use for this talent. She hadn't discovered many people with this talent, but still, she did not need anyone messing around in her head and discovering her secrets.

She had discovered her ability to "push" people a long time ago. Her ability to "probe" people was a recent discovery. These were talents that she worked very hard at *not* using. It was very tempting to use her talent to push someone to get her way, or to probe someone to see what they thought of her. But the idea of intruding on people's privacy in that manner was abhorrent to her and, except for the one occasion when she had pushed Master Teslan, she did not use these talents.

It did mean, however, that, in addition to maintaining an appearance illusion and monitoring her surroundings, she needed to maintain a mind barrier to prevent others from inadvertently discovering her secrets

Like the illusion talent, she would need to do this in such a way that people would be unaware she was doing so. However, accomplishing this would be a bit easier than masking the illusion. She knew there were people that had a natural ability to block any mind intrusions, so she just needed to mimic that natural talent.

And she would continue to work on discovering and mastering as many other new talents as she could.

CHAPTER 7

"Damn!" Squint felt a smack on the back of her head.

She was so intent on maintaining her appearance illusion and mind barrier that she had forgotten to monitor her surroundings, which had brought her across the path of Quellan Greves. Since this was Quellan's last term at the academy, he spent most of his time in Kenna, so she had gotten a bit lazy about keeping track of him. Now she was sure she was going to pay for it.

She turned to leave, and Quellan grabbed her arm and said "Well looky what I found. I haven't seen much of you. I thought maybe things here were too difficult for you and you quit the academy. Or has the little mouse been hiding in a hole somewhere?"

She tried to pull away, but he gripped her arm tighter.

"Aw, come one. I've learned something new, and I want to share it with you."

And with that, he let go of her arm, took a small step back, and flicked a hand in her direction. A small flame erupted from the hand and shot in her direction. She ducked, and the flame continued on behind her a short distance, before fading out.

"Isn't that fun?" he said. He flicked both hands and shot ice in her direction. "I can do fire, ice and wind, although I haven't found much use for the wind yet."

As she tried to evade the ice, she tripped and fell flat on her back, knocking the wind out of her. Quellan immediately took advantage. He viciously snapped both hands, and loosed a massive pair of fireballs in her direction.

What happened next was so quick that it was hard to follow.

As Quellan loosed the fireballs, she instinctively raised her hands in front of her to protect herself. This apparently triggered a shield of some kind that deflected the fireballs slightly up from where she lay.

At that moment, a laughing Young Donald and two other students came around the corner of the building. The fireballs slammed into Young Donald's chest, knocking him backwards. He was immediately engulfed in flames, and screamed as he fell to the ground. Within seconds, the only thing left of Young Donald was a pile of ash where he had fallen.

Quellan, whimpered. Looking at Squint, he whispered, "No, I didn't mean it," and fled.

Squint was still lying on the ground, too stunned to move. She had one hand on her chest, touching the birthday stone through her shirt. One of the students was standing in a daze, staring blankly at the pile of ashes, and the other was crying and screaming, "What did he do? What did he do?" over and over again.

Soon they were surrounded by a large crowd of students and teachers. Master Teslan was trying, not very successfully, to calm the screaming student, and one of the other teachers was trying to question the other student, who just continued to stare blankly at the ashes.

As Squint tried to rise, Headmaster McGillin offered her a hand, and helped her to her feet. He noticed Mistress Roseman nearby, and motioned her over. He asked her to take the two distraught students to his office and wait for him. He knew she would do her best to calm and comfort them while they waited.

Without letting go of Squint's hand, he announced to the crowd that everything was under control, and that they were to return to what they had been doing.

As the crowd broke up, Squint discreetly pointed to the pile of ashes, and whispered, "That's Young Donald."

The headmaster looked at her in shock. "What are you talking about, Squint? What the hell happened here?"

Realizing the state she was in, he said, "I'll have someone take care of the ashes. Right now, let's get inside where we can talk."

Knowing he could trust Master Teslan's discretion, the headmaster quickly explained what he knew of the situation to the librarian, and asked that he gather the ashes, to be given to Young Donald's family. He invited him to join them in his office once the task was complete.

Grateful for the comforting grip of Headmaster McGillin's hand, Squint tried not to think about Master Teslan's task as she and the headmaster went into the building. She couldn't believe Young Donald was gone. Just gone. And what about Quellan? Remembering his face just before he fled, she knew that he was horrified by what he had done. Where would he go? What would happen to him?

While waiting for them to arrive, Mistress Roseman had been her usual thoughtful and efficient self, and had arranged seating for everyone in a semi-circle in front of the fireplace. She was sitting with a boy on either side of her, and they were discussing, of all things, flavors of ice cream. Whatever she had done, the two boys appeared to be over their hysterics.

Squint and the headmaster took seats, and they introduced themselves while they waited for Master Teslan to join them.

The "screaming" boy said that his name was Beldon Heslan, he was fifteen years old, and this was his first term at the academy. He had been attending the local school in a small neighboring village, but had been bright enough that the schoolmaster had sent him to the academy, where he could get a more extensive education than his village could offer.

The other boy introduced himself as Vayan Dorn. He said he was also fifteen, was from Kenna, and had been attending the Kenna academy since he was twelve.

Squint said she was living with her grandmother just outside of Kenna, and she had been attending the academy for two years. She did not mention her age or her "special" status.

They all turned as Master Teslan entered. He nodded slightly to the headmaster, and seated himself.

"Okay, said McGillin, "Let's see if we can't sort out what just happened."

"It was that man. He threw fire at Young Donald!" said Vayan excitedly.

"Yes," agreed Beldon. "He just threw it right at him. We were going to the library, and when we came around the corner, he just threw fire right at Young Donald! For no reason!"

"And when he threw the fire, Squint here fell over," said Vayan. "Must have knocked the wind right out of him."

Squint was amazed at the difference in what the boys perceived had happened, and what she knew had happened. Apparently neither boy realized that she was already on the ground when Quellan threw the fireballs. They did not realize that she was the target, and they did not realize that she had deflected the fireballs that hit Young Donald.

It was also apparent that neither boy knew Quellan, and Quellan had fled before anyone else arrived.

Should she tell them that it was Quellan? She knew that what he did was a terrible thing. But she also knew that Quellan was aware of just how terrible it was, and that he was horrified by what he had done.

In addition, if she explained that it was Quellan, she would have to explain that he was aiming for her. How could she explain her deflection of the fireballs?

She was sure she would be unable to maintain her secret if she had to explain. If her secret came out, her discovery by the Magician was inevitable. He would come after her, and she was far too young and inexperienced to face him how. She would be quickly defeated, and there would be no one to defend the world against his hatred.

If she identified Quellan, they would catch him and put him away forever. Would that be right? He was genuinely sorry for what had happened, and she was as much to blame for the death as Quellan was. It was her deflection of the fireballs that had caused them to hit Young Donald.

In the end, Squint decided that, since Quellan was not entirely at fault for Young Donald's death, and she was unable to explain her part in the incident, she would agree with the boys' description of what happened, and remain silent about the identity of the man who precipitated the death of Young Donald.

One more secret to keep.

The following morning, when Squint arrived at Ancient Languages, her first class of the day, she was immediately surrounded by boys wanting information about yesterday's incident. What happened? Who was the man? Where had he gone? Was she hurt? Had she been frightened? What about the other boys? Did she know them? What was going to happen now? Would there be a manhunt?

When Master Rodine entered the classroom, the boys reluctantly went to their seats. They continued to glance furtively at Squint during the class, and as soon as Master Rodine dismissed the class, they once again surrounded Squint, peppering her with questions.

She found herself followed by boys all the way to her next class, which was just as full of questioning boys as the last. This continued through the rest of her morning. Squint was used to spending her days pretty much alone. She was definitely not happy about being thrust into the limelight like this, but she didn't know what she could do about it.

By lunchtime, she had had enough, and decided to join her grandmother in the kitchen, where the boys wouldn't follow. When she arrived, her grandmother was up to her elbows in flour, literally. She was kneading bread for tomorrow's lunch, and couldn't stop to talk to Squint.

Although it would have been nice to discuss her new-found status as the center of attention with her grandmother, Squint supposed it could wait until this evening. At least here, she was not being pestered. She grabbed a handful of carrots from the counter where lunch was being prepared, and found a quiet corner, out of the way of preparations, where she could sit and watch her grandmother run her kitchen.

When Squint had gotten home after the incident yesterday, she and her grandmother had discussed the death of Young Donald and Squint's role in it at length. When Squint stated that she was just as guilty as Quellan for the death, she thought her grandmother was going to smack her. Her grandmother half rose from her chair and yelled at Squint that she was an idiot to think that. Quellan was the one who was trying to hurt Squint. Squint had only been protecting herself. She was in no way responsible for the death of Young Donald.

Her grandmother had agreed with Squint's decision to keep quiet about Quellan's identity. She told Squint that preventing her discovery by the Magician was absolutely essential, and anything that could be done to aid in that goal must be done. It made Squint feel better about her decision.

When it was time to leave for her Advanced Mechanics class, Squint decided to try cloaking herself, so she wouldn't have to deal with all the questions. She stepped behind a shelf of food, and triggered the cloak. She carefully made her way out of the kitchen, and headed for class.

When she got to the classroom, she realized she had a small problem. There wasn't anywhere to uncloak without being seen. And there were so many boys around, she was having trouble not bumping into anyone. Maybe this hadn't been such a good idea.

She carefully worked her way back outside while trying to think of a solution. She finally resorted to hiding behind some bushes, uncloaking and walking out of the bushes like she hid behind bushes every day. She was immediately surrounded by questioning boys, none of whom appeared to think it odd that she had just emerged from the bushes.

For the second time since attending the academy, Squint was late for a class. As she entered the classroom, Master Jaydson gave her a knowing look and told her to take her seat. She self-consciously headed for her desk in the back of the classroom. On her way, she noticed Vayan Dorn, who nodded at her as she passed him. She hadn't realized that she shared a class with either of the boys involved in yesterday's incident. She nodded back and continued on to her seat.

When the class ended, she was once again surrounded by boys. Vayan, who was a rather large boy, pushed his way close to her, and said, "Come on, let's get out of here." He started shoving his way through the crowd, and Squint followed as closely as she could.

Once they maneuvered their way through the crowd and out the door, Vayan asked, "Do you have any more classes today?"

"No, I was going to go hide in the library," she said.

Vayan glanced at the crowd of boys surrounding them. "Beldon and I have been getting this same treatment. This was my last class, and Beldon's already done for the day. We're going to see if we can get permission to go to town to get away from all this craziness. Want to go with us?"

"Sounds great," she said, "as long as they don't decide to follow us."

Vayan grinned and said "We should lose them at the administration building. Beldon will be waiting inside."

As Vayan had predicted, once they entered the administration building, most of crowd had disappeared. As they headed for the headmaster's office, where Beldon was waiting, the last few boys wandered away.

"Hi, you going with us?" asked Beldon as they approached.

Beldon, although smaller than Vayan, was still taller than most boys his age. He had dark, curly hair and the beginnings of a full beard. Vayan was taller and broader than Beldon. He had blonde hair down to his shoulders, although he kept it tied back most of the time, and was clean-shaven.

Squint was three years younger than the other two, and small for her age, even for a girl. After much experimentation, she found that it was easiest to maintain an illusion that closely resembled reality, and because she was only twelve, there wasn't much about her appearance that needed to be changed. However, since the faculty had been led to believe she was fourteen, she altered her appearance to that of a smaller-than-normal fourteen-year-old boy, with short reddish-brown hair.

"Vayan invited me. Is that okay?" asked Squint.

"Why not," he said. "You appear to need to get out of here as much as we do."

The short conversation had apparently attracted the attention of Headmaster McGillin, who appeared in his open doorway.

"Good afternoon, gentlemen. Is there something I can do for you?"

"Can we talk to you, sir?" asked Squint.

The headmaster gestured to his office, and waited while the three entered. He shut the door and joined them at his desk.

"Now how can I help you?" he asked.

The two boys glanced at each other, and then looked at Squint.

Squint took the hint and said, "We've been having some problems with the other students pestering us for information about yesterday's incident. It's so bad that we can't get from place to place without being hounded. None of us have any classes for the rest of the day, so we were hoping you would give us permission to go to Kenna. We figure it will not only help us, but will help get things back to normal around here."

"I noticed the disruptions, and was wondering about them," Headmaster McGillin said. "Your plan sounds like a good idea. Squint, stop and see your grandmother before you leave campus. Vayan, you should stop at home while you're in town, and let your parents know what you're doing. Make sure you're all at home before dark."

As the three students rose to leave, the headmaster said, "Remember that you are representatives of this academy and behave accordingly. Stay out of trouble."

As they left the office, Vayan turned to Squint and said, "Hey, thanks for doing the talking. Let's get out of here, before we get mobbed again."

Leaving the building with some trepidation, the three looked around and realized that most of the students were in class now, so they shouldn't be bothered.

"Let's head for town while it's clear," said Beldon, quickening his step.

"Wait," said Squint. "We have to stop by the kitchen first."

"What?" said Beldon "Why?" said Vayan.

"I have to talk to my grandmother before we go," she said.

"In the kitchen?" asked Vayan.

It suddenly occurred to her that the two boys might find it beneath them to be associating with the cook's grandson, but there was nothing she could do about it. If they had a problem with it, she could always go to Kenna by herself.

"She's the head cook," she responded. "Maybe, if we're really nice, she'll find us something to eat."

"Sounds great," said Vayan, with a grin.

"Yeah, but let's make it quick, before we get mobbed again," said Beldon.

Breathing a sigh of relief, Squint trotted to keep up with the boys as they headed for the kitchen. She led them around to the back of the building, where they could enter directly into the kitchen, avoiding any chance of meeting students in the cafeteria.

They were greeted with shouts of, "Hey, Squint," and "Who're your new friends, Squint," and "What's going on, Squint," as they entered the kitchen.

"You seem to be popular," commented Vayan. "I take it you come here a lot?"

'Yeah, I usually meet my grandmother here at the end of the day. We live close by, and we walk home together." She grinned. "And someone usually has a special treat for me."

Vayan grinned back and said, "That would make me want to walk home with my grandmother, too. And I don't even like my grandmother."

Her grandmother, entering from the cafeteria, said, "Why, what's wrong with your grandmother?"

"Hi, gramma," said Squint. She gestured at Beldon, and said "This is Beldon Heslan, and the one who doesn't like his grandmother is Vayan Dorn. This is my grandmother, Cayrah Nylls."

Mrs. Nylls looked at Vayan. "Is your grandmother Nella Dorn?"

Vayan nodded.

"That explains it. Now, what are you children doing here at this time of day. Shouldn't you be in class?"

Squint glanced around and lowered her voice. "These are the boys that were involved in the incident yesterday. We've been mobbed all day by kids asking questions about what happened. Headmaster McGillin gave us permission to go to Kenna. Is that all right?"

"Sounds like a sensible plan. Sounds like fun, too. I'll make you some lunch before you go. Squint, you can stop by the house and take those books you borrowed back to Mr. Johnson, if you want." She winked at them and said, "There's still some chocolate cake left on the counter, if you have room after lunch."

Mrs. Nylls set them up with lunch at the small table in the back of the kitchen that Squint normally occupied while she waited for her grandmother to finish up in the kitchen for the day.

During their lunchtime conversation, Squint discovered that both boys loved to read, and they both knew Mr. Johnson and his books very well. The boys were surprised that Mr. Johnson was willing to lend books to Squint. They had both spent time at this shop reading, but neither had been allowed to take books home.

She learned that the two boys had been friends for most of their time at academy. They were both bookworms, and both consistently earned top marks in their classes. Unlike most of the students, they actually enjoyed studying.

They were enjoying their conversation so much, they decided to spend enough time in the kitchen for the current class to end and the next class to begin before they headed out. They would start their trip to town by stopping at Squint's house for some cake and to gather Squint's borrowed books. The next stop would be Vayan's house to let his family know what they were doing. Then they would be off to visit the bookseller. After that, they would just take things as they came.

And so it went. They thoroughly enjoyed eating the last of the leftover cake. Squint and Beldon were introduced to Vayan's family, including his very unpleasant grandmother.

Squint was amazed that her younger age didn't seem to make any difference to the boys. They were having a great time. At least they were until they left Mr. Johnson's shop.

And there, as big as life and as loud as ever, was Mr. Bronday, yelling at a street vendor. The boys looked at him, and Vayan muttered, "Not again."

Squint glanced at him, and he said, "That pompous loudmouth thinks he's better than everyone."

And just like that, Squint decided to let the two boys in on just a tiny bit of her secret.
"If I show you something, do you promise to keep it to yourself?" she asked.

They both looked at her with interest.

"As long as it's something good," said Vayan.

"Yeah, we need some excitement," agreed Beldon.

Looking at them slyly, she said, "That loudmouth is Mr. Bronday. He's the mayor of the village I grew up in. I have a small talent that no one knows about. Shall we make use of it to entertain Mr. Bronday?" she asked.

Catching on to her look, Vayan said, "Go for it. We'll keep your talent to ourselves." Beldon nodded in agreement.

Keeping slightly behind the boys, Squint watched as Mr. Bronday thrust a bag at the street vendor in front of him, and shouted. "Look at these," he shouted," is this what I asked for? NO. I said I wanted DARK chocolates. BIG dark chocolates. Not these tiny little things. Now take these back and give me what I asked for!" He waited, fuming, while the vendor chose some chocolates, bagged them, and handed them to him.

"Hmph," he snorted. "I suppose these will do, but I shouldn't have to pay full price for them." He tossed some coins on the man's cart, and strutted away.

Squint grinned at the boys, and said, "Okay, let's follow him and see if we can't give him what he's asking for."

They wandered along behind Mr. Bronday until he neared a group of dogs. Squint glanced at the boys, and said "Now."

All of a sudden, Mr. Bronday shouted, "What the hell," and jump-stepped to the side. It appeared the bag he was carrying had torn, and his chocolates were all over the ground.

The nearby dogs arrived immediately, to made short work of Mr. Bronday's big, dark chocolates.

The three, laughing loudly, ducked into the nearest store.

Beldon said, "I don't know why you have chosen to keep this talent to yourself, but I think we should spend our day using it to entertain your friend."

And that's how the three of them spent the next few hours, until Mr. Bronday had enough and went home.

Mr. Bronday fell into a puddle, dropped and broke a small statuette he had just purchased, accidently knocked his plate of food to the ground, and experienced several other little mishaps that the three new friends found highly amusing.

Although Squint wanted nothing more than to see Mr. Bronday pay for what he had done to her family, she was very pleased that neither boy suggested that they do anything more than play pranks on him. It made her more comfortable about having shared a bit of her secret with them.

She found it interesting that neither boy questioned why she kept her small talent secret, but was grateful that she didn't have to concoct an explanation.

The three spent the rest of the afternoon wandering around Kenna and getting to know each other better. They thoroughly enjoyed themselves, and were disappointed when dusk came and they had to end the day.

CHAPTER 8

From that day forward, Squint's days changed drastically. She was spending most of her free time with Vayan and Beldon. Although the three enjoyed studying together, they spent most of their leisure time on leisure activities, which was a new experience for Squint. There was a myriad of activities available for the boys at the academy, and the three availed themselves of most of them.

As the three got to know each other better, Squint discovered that Vayan and Beldon had one talent each. Vayan's talent allowed him to enhance his physical abilities for short periods, becoming faster, stronger and more coordinated. Beldon was able to increase and decrease the level of his senses. This included his ability to see and hear, his sensitivity to pain, heat and cold, and control of his equilibrium. Unfortunately, he was unable to control which senses he heightened or reduced, which made his talent rather useless.

One of their favorite activities involved Squint's use of the talent she had shared with them in Kenna the day after Young Donald's death.

Initially, Squint had been concerned that one of them would betray her secret. However, there was an occasion when Beldon started to discuss the events in Kenna, and Vayan had "accidently" bumped into him. Hard. He had given Beldon a dirty look and said, "We had a good time that day. Didn't really do that much."

Later, when the three were alone, Beldon said, "Geez, Vayan why'd you smack me? I was just going to tell him about Squint getting to borrow books from Mr. Johnson." And with that, Squint knew her secret was safe.

On most nice days, students would gather in the field behind the cafeteria for a game of squares. The game was so popular at the academy that the field was permanently marked for the game. It had a square drawn the full size of the field. This square was marked with a small square in the center and one at each of the four corners. Each of the five smaller squares is just big enough to hold four players without touching.

The game of squares requires nine to twenty players. The players are split into four equal groups, one for each corner. The rest of the players go to the center square, with a maximum number of four players in any square. The players in the corner squares are called pillars; the players in the center are called pins. Although the rules require a minimum of two pillars in each square, it is often played with fewer.

At the beginning of the game, the hands of the pillars are lightly bound behind their backs, and the pins are each given a "box," which is a cube of leather filled with lightly-packed feathers, just the right size to fit in a person's hand.

All players begin counting together. At the count of four—the number of sides on a square—the pin or pins all throw their box at any pillar of their choosing. Pillars are allowed to move and duck to avoid boxes, as long as they stay within their square. Any pillar who steps (or falls) out of his square is out of the game. Any pillar who is hit by a box is out of the game.

Once all boxes have hit the ground, the pins recover their boxes and return to the center square, and the next round begins. The object of the game is to be the last pillar.

Intentional pushing and shoving of fellow pillars is not allowed, and means immediate disqualification. The use of talents is strictly forbidden. Use of either pretty much guarantees that a player will be labeled a cheater and won't be allowed to play again, so neither is employed very often.

It takes a good deal of practice to be able to throw the box with any accuracy. There is nothing aerodynamic about a cube, and the fact that it is so light makes it difficult to keep it going the same direction in which it is aimed. If the pins all choose to throw at the same pillar, and they are all good at aiming the box, it makes for some interesting scrambling in the aimed-at square. Trying to avoid a box without shoving other pillars in the square can really challenge a pillar's balance.

Although Beldon and Vayan enjoyed the game, they rarely participated. Beldon was shy enough to be uncomfortable participating in spectator sports, and Vayan felt his size and the nature of his talent gave him an unfair advantage. Squint, of course, had always been too busy with her studies to participate.

The three friends would sit on a hill overlooking the playing field. With all attention focused on the game, the three would focus on the spectators. They would search for someone who was being particularly unpleasant and give them the same type of attention they had given Mr. Bronday in Kenna. Never anything really hurtful, just annoying. Spilling drinks, dropping food, tripping. Squint found she could even make small bugs swarm a particular place, or birds splat on target.

They found it highly entertaining, and it usually meant that the annoying student left and made the game more pleasant for others.

Since starting at the academy, at the end of each day, Squint would meet her grandmother in the kitchen, and the two would walk home together. After the incident, she discovered that Vayan also went to his home in Kenna to have dinner and spend the night with his family.

Beldon, on the other hand, had dinner in the cafeteria, and slept in his room in the northern-most of the two academy dormitories. Unlike Vayan, who got along with everyone, Beldon was quieter and spent most of his evenings in solitary activities.

Shortly after learning of this, as they sat down for their dinner one evening, Squint told her grandmother that she felt sad for Beldon, having no one to eat dinner or spend his evenings with. She immediately got the response she was hoping for.

"You tell that young man to come to the cafeteria with you tomorrow. He can come home with us for dinner. No one should eat a meal by themselves. Food tastes much better when you share it with friends."

And so Beldon began spending most evenings at the Nylls home. Vayan occasionally joined them, and the four would spend lively evenings discussing whatever they found interesting at the moment. Squint would often choose an opposing opinion about the current topic, just to keep the discussion lively.

In addition to bringing about the new friendship between the three students, the incident with Quellan Greves had another, more practical benefit. It made Squint and her grandmother realize that she was neglecting an important area of magic during her training. She needed to add defensive magic to her practice sessions.

This took a bit more creativity. To practice defensive magic, she needed something to defend against. Her grandmother was able to help with physical defense by throwing things at her and trying to attack her, but Squint mastered defending against these attacks very quickly. She would eventually need to find a way to work on this at a higher level, but they both assumed that the Magician would use magic, rather than physical attacks. She needed to find a way to practice defending against magic.

After a great many attempts, she found that she could "bounce" her magic attacks off the walls at the magic center. This sent her magic careening around the room, giving her an opportunity to practice creating and controlling her magic, defending against the magic she created, and dispersing it once she was finished.

With her grandmother sheltered behind the safety barriers, she worked on controlling the initial direction and strength of various types of magic. She also worked on changing the properties of magic once it was launched, weakening or strengthening it, and changing its course.

CHAPTER 9

For the next three years, the three friends spent most of their free time together. By the time Beldon and Vayan reached their final year at the academy and began making plans for the future, the three had become inseparable.

They had become such good friends that Squint had even considered sharing her secrets with them. However, although she trusted them absolutely, she was worried that one of them might accidently give something away. For now, she would keep things as they were.

Beldon had applied to teach mathematics at the academy, and had been accepted. His family didn't have a lot of money, and this would allow him to help them out in a much better way than anything he could do if he went home.

Vayan was to join his family's furniture business in Kenna. Although he was the youngest of three boys, neither of his older brothers was interested in woodworking, and both had moved to bigger towns in the hope of finding something that better suited their temperaments. Although Vayan felt obligated to help his father, he also enjoyed woodworking, and was very adept at making furniture. He was quite happy in Kenna, and had no desire to move away.

These arrangements suited the three friends fine, since it meant that they would be able to continue to spend time together after the older two left the academy.

In addition to spending several evenings a week at the Nylls house, the two boys often joined Squint and her grandmother on their Saturday shopping trips into Kenna. Or, rather, Squint and Beldon walked to Kenna with Mrs. Nylls, where the two friends met with Vayan, and then spent the day together. They would all meet for lunch, and at the end of the day, Beldon, Squint and Mrs. Nylls would walk to the Nylls home together, and Beldon would continue on to the academy.

The one blight on her life during this period was that Squint often saw Mr. Bronday in town, sometimes with his family. She was no longer afraid that he would recognize her, but there was something in her that hated seeing him in town spending time with his family. It made her want to hurt him like he had hurt her. And that made her even angrier at him for making her feel that way.

Since Squint spent so much time in the library, Master Teslan had made her one of his library assistants. Like Young Donald had in the past, Squint and the two other student assistants kept the library in order. They returned books to their shelves, helped students find the books they wanted, and did general cleaning duties.

In early dwowen, Master Teslan announced that he would be arranging a trip to visit the academy in Melsta, the capitol city. All students in their final year would be invited, giving them a chance to see the capitol city, and perhaps helping them with the decision they would soon be making about what they wanted to do with their lives. The academy would be paying all expenses, so it was an opportunity that many of the students could never manage on their own.

Shortly after making the announcement, Master Teslan took Squint aside and told her that, since the two other library assistants were both in their final year and were included in the invitation, he felt that she, too, should be included. He offered her the opportunity to join them.

Squint was very excited at the prospect of going to Melsta Academy. She and her grandmother discussed the trip, especially the logistics of Squint traveling to the capitol as a boy. This would entail her sharing a room with other boys, which meant sleeping in the same room. Squint was pretty sure she could work around the obvious problems, but she was reasonably sure that she could not get past the fact that she could not maintain the change in her appearance while she slept.

Now that she was getting older, Squint found that she liked feeling feminine. Since she spent most of her time looking like a boy, she wanted something that would let her feel pretty. She had let her hair grow, and it was now almost to her waist. In addition to making her feel pretty, the feel of it on her back was a constant reminder to keep vigil on her appearance.

Her grandmother told her that it reminded her of Squint's mother, which just added to the pleasure it gave Squint to feel it on her back.

During the day, in addition to making it appear short, she kept it braided tightly and tucked into her clothing, so that it couldn't swing free and give her away.

Since the changes she made to her appearance were relatively minor, she could probably manage to avoid discovery on the trip, but there would be no hiding her hair. Cutting it short would solve that problem, but she wasn't sure a trip to the capitol was worth losing her one vanity.

Several weeks after he issued the invitation, Master Teslan found Squint alone in the library. He mentioned that she had not responded to the invitation to Melsta, and asked if there was a problem.

"Well," she said, "My grandmother is concerned about me traveling with so many boys older than I am. She's worried that they might have a bad influence on me."

"I think I can ease her mind about that," responded Master Teslan. "I can assure her that I will personally keep an eye on you." He thought for a moment, and then said, "I'm sure I can also arrange for you to have a room of your own at Melsta Academy, which should alleviate her concerns. I can speak to her directly, if you think that would help. I really think this trip is something that would be perfect for you, Squint."

Squint said, "Oh, if I can tell her that you'll be keeping an eye on me and I won't be sharing a room, I'm sure she'll let me go."

Beldon and Vayan also received permission to visit Melsta, and the three spent hours talking about what they wanted to do and see while they were in the capitol city, and wondering how much freedom they would be given.

Squint's grandmother frequently reminded the three that Squint would be under Master Teslan's direct supervision, and was not likely to be given much freedom, but this did not dampen their enthusiasm.

CHAPTER 10

On the day of departure, the three met at Vayan's home in Kenna, and walked together to the train station. Although each student was allowed to take two suitcases with them, all three friends had managed to pack enough for the week-long trip into one case each. This left them plenty of room to bring back any souvenirs and gifts they might pick up on the trip in the second case they brought with them.

Mrs. Nylls and Mr. Dorn, Vayan's father, had been very generous with funds for the trip. Since Beldon's family had little money, Mrs. Nylls and Mr. Dorn had both made sure that Beldon would also have enough to buy whatever caught his eye.

The scene at the train station was one of chaos. There were seventy or so students milling about and shouting to each other. Master Teslan and the three teachers chosen to help supervise were attempting to check off names on the list of students with permission to take the trip, and to make sure no one boarded the train who was not on the list.

The train was being provided by the Melsta Academy, and had only three cars; a passenger car, a dining car, and a freight car that held goods being sent to various stops along their route. The students boarded the dining car, and were shepherded through to the passenger car. It took nearly an hour to get everyone on the train and ready to leave.

And they were finally on their way! For the first hour or so, Squint sat next to a window, thoroughly engrossed with watching the scenery flow by. She had been too excited to sleep much the night before, and was finally unwinding. Just sitting and enjoying the view was enough for her right now.

Beldon and Vayan had been wandering among the other students. They joined Squint at her seat, and the three spent a while just enjoying being together and watching the scenery. Students were beginning to wander towards the dining car, and the three decided to go see what was being offered.

They shared a table with several other students, and the conversation was lively. The three friends were defending their opinion that Squint's grandmother was a better cook than whoever prepared today's food. It didn't take them long to win the argument, especially after mentioning the chocolate strawberry cakes she made for special occasions.

The conversation turned to the trip and their expectations. One of the students mentioned the night they would be spending at the academy in the City of Rayne. Rayne sat at the edge of the Great River. Here, they would transfer to the ferry to cross the river, before continuing on by train to Melsta.

Squint had known that they would be transferring to the ferry in Rayne. She had not known they would be spending the night at the academy there. Master Teslan had assured her grandmother that she would have her own accommodations at the academy in Melsta. Nothing had been said about Rayne.

She spent the rest of the trip to Rayne worrying about how she would deal with the situation if she had to share a room at the academy.

Because it was late evening when the train arrived at the City of Rayne, the students were ushered directly to the academy.

The city was about half the size of Melsta, but still enormous compared to Kenna. Unlike the Kenna Academy, which was situated just outside of the town, the Rayne Academy was in the heart of town. The large group of students drew a lot of attention as they made their way—slowly, with many stops to gawk at the sites—to their destination.

Once they arrived at the academy, the students were separated and sent to various dormitories for the night. Beldon and Vayan were in a different group than the one to which Squint was assigned. As she had feared, Squint was assigned to one of the dormitory rooms, and was not given a room of her own.

After her restless night last night, she knew she would be unable to stay awake. Maintaining her appearance illusion while she slept would be impossible. She really wasn't sure what she was going to do.

When they arrived at their room, the students each found a large robe on their bed, along with a note welcoming the visiting students to the Rayne Academy for the Talented. The robes were midnight blue with silver trim, the academy colors. When Squint lifted hers, she discovered that it was designed with a cowl. Perfect! She could pull the cowl over her head while she slept, and keep her hair hidden. The robe was large enough to cover anything else she needed to hide.

She hid herself in the bathroom long enough to allow the other students in the room to be changed and ready for bed, and then returned to the room. In the morning, she again hid in the bathroom until the rest of the students had dressed and left the room, and then dressed and went to meet Beldon and Vayan.

As she made her way to the cafeteria, where they had been instructed to meet, Squint thought about how lucky she had been last night. Without the robe provided by the academy, she wasn't sure that she would have made it through the night without being "unmasked".

She had also been lucky in her ability to hide in the bathroom undetected while the fifteen or sixteen boys who shared her room undressed. She had no desire to become a voyeur.

Although they were being allowed to take the robes with them, Squint was still concerned about what was going to happen while they were in Melsta, if Master Teslan was unable to arrange private accommodations for her.

She was one of the last students to reach the cafeteria, and she was amazed at the number students and the amount of noise they were making. Having taken all her meals with her grandmother, either at home or in the academy kitchen, she had never eaten at the cafeteria in Kenna, so this was a new experience for her. But she was also relatively certain there were more people in this one room than the entire population of Kenna and its academy combined.

She managed to get herself a tray with some breakfast, and turned to search for Vayan or Beldon, or both. Vayan's size should make him fairly easy to spot. Luckily, they were seated together, fairly close to where she was, and there was room at the table for her to join them.

After enjoying a leisurely meal, the Kenna students were guided to the auditorium. There, they were told they would be assigned to one of four groups. Each group would be assigned to Master Teslan or one of the three instructors traveling with them. The groups would be given two hours to explore the academy and the surrounding town.

Once again, Squint found herself separated from Vayan and Beldon. This time, however, she protested. If she was going exploring, she wanted to share the experience with her friends. As it turned out, she was not the only one to protest their group assignment. After much shuffling about, everyone was satisfied with their assignment, and the various groups headed off to explore.

As expected, Master Teslan insisted on Squint being in his group, so Vayan and Beldon had joined her. This suited all three, since they enjoyed the librarian's company. They were sure they would have enjoyed themselves with whichever group they had been assigned, but they were glad it was to be Master Teslan.

And as they had hoped, the librarian's choice as their first stop was the academy library. Before leaving the auditorium, Master Teslan told the group that they would have one half hour to explore the library. He asked that they do so quietly, and with as little disturbance to library users as possible.

Unlike the Kenna library, which shared a building with the administration offices and first level classrooms, the library at Rayne occupied an entire building, which was larger than the administration building at Kenna. The building was two stories high, and was completely filled with enormous bookshelves. There were stools and ladders everywhere, providing easy access to upper shelves. In the center of the building was the largest spiral staircase Squint and her friends had ever seen.

Also unlike the Kenna library, there were people everywhere, both students and teachers, quietly bustling about.

The three spent the next half hour wandering through the shelves with Master Teslan, who was happy to point out its special features. The library, despite its size, was just as well organized as the Kenna library, and had several areas that contained special collections. Some of the collections had been donated by academy alumni or parents, and some had been collected over many years by academy librarians.

This library, like the Kenna library, had a restricted area. It was at least ten times the size of the restricted area at Kenna, and just as well protected. Of course visitors were not allowed in this area, but Master Teslan said that it contained a large number of books on runes and magical rituals. He said this collection was the pride of the academy, and was the largest and most comprehensive collection of its kind in the world. Squint carefully examined the area, thinking she would probably return here, if she decided to incorporate high magics into her studies.

In much too short a time, as far as the three were concerned, they returned to the doors of the library to meet with the rest of the group. Once everyone had gathered, they headed outside the academy to see what the town had to offer.

The weather was perfect. It was comfortably warm, with a light breeze, with no clouds to be seen.

For the next hour, the group roamed around the town, stopping here and there to visit stores and to allow students to marvel at the sites.

The three friends were more fascinated by the people than they were by the buildings and shops. Back home in Kenna, where goods were limited, people more or less dressed the same. Here, there was no end to the variety.

Beldon pointed out a man wandering around on ice skates, even though the weather was warm, and there was no ice to be seen anywhere. Vayan pointed out an older gentleman in one of the shops who appeared to be wearing nothing but his undergarments. Squint pointed out a man with a pair of work pants, topped by what looked like a table cloth with a hole cut in it for his head to go through.

They saw a woman who looked like she had an animal curled up on her head. They had an animated discussion about whether it was a hat, the woman's hair, or actually an animal. And if it was an animal, what kind.

There was a family--mother, father and three young children--wearing identical dresses. They all worked hard to stifle their laughter at a women carrying a small, curly-haired dog, who had her hair cut and colored to match the dog.

Several times, Squint felt a gentle touch on her mind. The touches were brief, and none were repeated. The touches felt like the ones she often experienced at home. And like home, there didn't appear to be any reaction to her barrier, so she hoped this meant she was successful in imitating a natural barrier.

CHAPTER 11

Finally, it was time to head for the ferry to meet with the other groups, and continue on to Melsta.

The trip on the ferry would take about an hour. It took nearly that long to get everyone on board. Once boarded, a handful of students went downstairs, but most stayed topside to enjoy the trip across the river.

The crossing was beautiful, but uneventful. Once across the river, it took another hour for everyone to disembark and board the train that was waiting for them. This last leg of their trip took a bit less than two hours.

Like the academy in Rayne, the Melsta Academy was in the center of town. Unlike their trek through Rayne, very few people in Melsta took any notice of the large group of students making its way through town.

They soon passed through a huge set of arches into an area of town where all the buildings were built in the same style, and few people were to be seen in the streets. It wasn't until they were ushered inside one of the larger buildings that the students realized this wasn't part of the town, but was actually the academy campus.

The Melsta Academy for the Talented was the largest of the academy's campuses. In fact, it was the largest school in the world. It was nearly as big as the town of Kenna, with over 8,000 students and staff.

Once inside the building, they were greeted by a small group of students, who escorted them to a huge auditorium. Inside, the curtains were pulled shut across the stage. They were seated in the front, center section, and were told someone would be with them shortly.

Instead, the curtains opened, and they were presented with a stage full of fancifully-dressed people--students, judging by their ages. There were all manner of animals of fable, characters from children's stories, and many other incredible costumes.

A large, pink Markin—one of the characters from the Doctor Dan stories—stepped forward. He (or she) welcomed the students with a hearty "Hello!" and began a lengthy poem of greeting. Each of the characters present on the stage was mentioned at some point in the poem, at which time they would frolic around the stage, doing stunts or behaving quite outrageously. Both the poem and the antics of the characters were hilarious.

Once the poem was finished, the Markin waved to the still laughing audience and said, in a loud "conspiratorial whisper" that was heard throughout the auditorium, that the visiting students were to be thanked for having provided the students and faculty of the Melsta Academy for the Talented with an unplanned, three-day holiday. For the duration of the Kenna student's stay, the Melsta Academy was suspending classes.

Once again, the Kenna students were asked to break into groups. This time, however, the groups were to be no bigger than five students each. Each group would be accompanied by a Melsta teacher, chosen from lists of names organized by interest.

The three Kenna teachers were going to be given a break from supervising and would be choosing their own Melsta teacher to show them around.

Students milled about, trying to find suitable groups. There were lists of teachers with all types of interests, including stage, music, history, even a list of teachers whose primary interest was the game of squares.

Once a group was formed, and the choice of guide made, the name would be taken to the young man who had played the Markin. The Markin, better known as Nevra Senner, head of the student council, would then send one of the student performers to bring the selected teacher to meet the group of students.

If after meeting the teacher, they found they were not compatible, they were free to select a different name from the lists. If they seemed compatible, the newly-formed group was to go on to the dining hall, where dinner was currently being served. They would have dinner together, allowing them to get to know each other better.

After dinner, everyone would meet in the academy's social center to either finalize their choice, or to select another teacher. For the rest of the evening, the groups would spend time in the center, getting to know their guides.

Nevra would be around all evening to help ensure that all of the groups ended up with someone that suited them. The Melsta Academy wanted to ensure that everyone had the best possible experience for the remainder of their visit.

While the groups were still getting organized, Squint mentioned to Vayan and Beldon that Master Teslan seemed to be left without a group. The three decided to ask Master Teslan if he would like to join their group.

They tracked him down, and invited him to join their group. He replied solemnly that, since he had promised to personally look after Squint, he was more or less required to accompany them. He then grinned hugely, and said that he would like nothing better than to spend his time in Melsta with them.

Adding the librarian to their group turned out to be a great boon for the three students. As they were perusing the lists to find a guide, a gentleman approached Master Teslan. He introduced himself as Master Peyta, Head Librarian of the Melsta Academy, and offered his services as a guide to the City of Melsta, including its many libraries.

Master Teslan introduced the three Kenna students as his companions for the trip. Master Peyta asked the four to join him for dinner. After dinner, if they were agreeable, he would list himself as their guide for the remainder of the trip.

Over dinner, they found out that Master Peyta was the youngest of the academies' master librarians. This was his first term in that role, and he was thoroughly enjoying his new position. They also discovered that he had a great sense of humor and seemed to fit into their little group quite well.

Among the many things they discussed at dinner was the sleeping arrangements for the Kenna visitors while they were in town. As it turned out, there was a newly-built housing unit that, although complete, was not yet occupied. This building would provide the accommodations for them during their stay. Although the rooms were big enough to be shared, there were enough rooms for each student and teacher to have a room of their own, if they chose.

This, of course, was a great relief to Squint, who was now able to quit worrying about that aspect of the trip and could concentrate on having a good time.

After dinner, the five of them found a quiet corner in the social center, where they spent a very pleasant evening getting to know each other better. It was clear that, like Master Teslan, Master Peyta had a wide variety of interests and was very knowledgeable about a number of subjects.

At the end of a very enjoyable day, Master Peyta escorted them to the housing unit where they would be spending their nights. The building was much bigger than they expected. Master Peyta told them that it had 115 rooms. The Kenna visitors were being given their choice of rooms in the five-story building.

When the librarian mentioned that some of the rooms were arranged for multiple students, Vayan immediately asked if there was a room that would allow him, Beldon and Squint to share.

Before Master Peyta could answer, Master Teslan reminded Squint that he had promised Mrs. Nylls that Squint would not be sharing a room.

Vayan groaned and said, "Well isn't that just lovely. Can he at least have a room next to us?"

"Yes," replied Master Teslan, "and I'll have the one on the other side of his. So, if you can find us three rooms together, Master Peyta, that would be perfect."

In the entryway of the building, a chart had been set up showing the layout of the building. The rooms had spaces for names to be written to indicate that they had been claimed. It appeared that about half of the rooms had already been selected.

After choosing three rooms together on the fifth floor, Master Teslan said that he wanted to stay downstairs and make sure all of the Kenna students and teachers were settled in for the night before he turned in. Master Peyta offered to stay with him, so the three students said good night to the librarians and headed upstairs.

They went into the boys' room first. It was a beautiful room, with a great view of the campus. It was set up to accommodate two students, with a bed, dresser and desk on each side of the room. It had all of the newest amenities, including a small kitchen.

Vayan flopped his suitcase onto one of the beds, and said, "Hey, Beldon. This one's mine, okay?"

Beldon shrugged, and said, "They both look pretty comfortable to me," and dropped his suitcase beside the other bed.

Vayan said, "I'm going to put on the robe I got in Rayne," and started removing his clothing.

Squint said, "Well, I should head for my room," and started for the door.

"What's the deal with you, Squint," asked Vayan. "You always do that."

"What?" Asked Squint without turning around, although she was pretty sure she knew what Vayan was talking about.

"Disappear as soon as anyone starts to undress. It's like you're afraid of what you'll see, or something," said Vayan with a grin.

Fingering her birthday stone for comfort, Squint gazed at Vayan and Beldon, seriously considering sharing her secrets with the two of them. All of her secrets. They had proven that they could keep a secret when they chose not to share that she had a talent. But that was a small secret compared to the rest of what she was considering sharing.

As she continued to wrestle with the decision, Vayan said, "Hey, what's with you. Stop staring at me like that, it's creepy."

In addition to the possibility of her secret getting out to others, she was afraid telling them that she was a girl would ruin their friendship. She had never had real friends before, and she didn't want to lose them.

And that was what made her decide. If she was really their friend, she should trust them with her secrets. And she really wanted to be able to be her true self around them, and if she couldn't, then she wasn't really their friend.

She took a big breath and abruptly dropped her appearance illusion. At the same time, she pulled her braid out of her shirt, and over her shoulder, so it dropped down her chest.

Vayan started to say something else to her, and then noticed the change in her appearance. Beldon had been quicker to notice the change, and was staring at her with his mouth open and a stunned looked on his face.

Vayan squinted at her, and said, "What did you just do? How did you do that? Why do you look like that?" He realized he was babbling, stopped talking and plopped down on the bed.

Squint moved to a couch and said, "Can you guys come sit down, so we can talk?"

Vayan just sat on the bed, staring at Squint, but Beldon headed for the couch with a grin on his face.

"I can't wait to hear your story," he said.

Vayan looked at Beldon, appeared to think about this comment for a moment, gave Squint a look, and said, "Okay, let's hear it."

And so she told them. Everything. Well, nearly everything. She decided not to include her encounters with Quellan Greves. She felt guilty enough over Young Donald's death during their final confrontation that she couldn't bring herself to share that with them. She also left out that she was so much younger than they were, although she wasn't sure why.

It took her nearly two hours to share everything else with them, including the trepidation she was feeling about sharing with them. Beldon had asked several questions during the telling, but Vayan had listened in complete silence.

At the end of her story, Beldon moved to sit beside her. He pulled her to him in a hug, and said, "Geez, I can't even imagine trying to keep all that a secret."

Vayan, on the other hand, just sat staring at her in silence. He had no expression on his face, so she couldn't judge what he was feeling.

Becoming really concerned by his lack of reaction, Squint finally said, "Vayan, are you upset with me?"

Vayan continued to stare at her for a few more moments. Suddenly, he jumped up from the bed, rushed over and grabbed Squint off the couch. He lifted her into the air and swung around and around with her held aloft in front of him. Just as suddenly, he set her down, dropped to the couch and grinned hugely at his two bewildered friends.

Both Squint and Beldon were looking at him like he'd lost his mind. Maybe he had. It certainly looked like he had.

Squint sat beside him on the couch and touched his shoulder. "Vayan, are you okay?" she asked.

He glanced at Beldon, turned to Squint, and said, "I love you, Squint."

Squint blinked at him in surprise, and Beldon snorted with laughter, "You love him? I mean her," he said.

"Oh, you have no idea," Vayan responded. "Now, let *me* explain," he said, and patted the couch beside him. "Come sit down and I'll tell you *my* secret."

Vayan explained that, during the time that they had been friends, he had been "seeing" things. He would see a blur around Squint, and then it would be gone. He would see her in one place, and then instantly in another. He thought he was losing his mind.

He said that, since they always seemed to revolve around Squint, he thought it might be a side effect of Squint's talent, even though that didn't really make sense. But nobody else seemed to notice, so he was afraid it was something wrong with him. As time went on, he saw them less and less often, so he thought that whatever was wrong with him must be getting better. He still worried about it, though.

Now, knowing the truth about Squint, he was incredibly relieved to know there was nothing wrong with him.

Vayan might feel better, but his story concerned Squint greatly. If Vayan, with no talent to "see" things, was still catching glimpses of her blur, she did not have the illusion perfected, like she thought she did. It was possible that someone with a real talent might see, not only the blur, but right through her disguise to her real self.

She didn't really care if most people could tell she was disguising herself. The disguise was pretty much there for one person. The Magician. If someone at the academy discovered her secret, it would be awkward, but not devastating. However, if the Magician were to discover her now, it would be catastrophic. She was nowhere near ready for a confrontation. Discovery at this point would mean certain death for her, and ruination for the world.

Realizing she could now share this concern with her friends, she did just that. Beldon mournfully stated that, if he could just learn to control his talent, he'd be able to tell her if her "blur was showing". The way he put it made them all laugh, lightening their mood considerably.

Vayan asked Squint if she thought there was some way she could help Beldon learn to control his talent.

She thought about it a moment, and said, "Well, it seems that learning to control which sense you choose to enhance should be about the same as what I've been doing with some of my talents. I can certainly show you what I've been doing, and we can see if it works for you." She grinned at Beldon, and said, "And maybe you can help me learn that talent."

"But not tonight," she said. "I'm sleepy, and I don't want to be too tired to enjoy whatever is planned for tomorrow." She gave each of the boys a big hug, and went to her own room.

Squint's trepidation over having shared her secret made it difficult for her to get to sleep. She was reasonably certain that neither boy would give her away deliberately, but there would be many opportunities for them to give her away accidently. She finally got to sleep by reminding herself that there was nothing she could do about it now. As the saying goes, "What's done is done." She had to trust her own instincts that she had done the right thing.

CHAPTER 12

She woke late the next morning to a quiet knocking at her door. She put on her illusion and her robe from Rayne Academy, and went to see who was there.

It was the two master librarians. They had identical frowns on their faces, and both started speaking at once. They quit speaking and looked at each other. If Squint hadn't been so tired, she would have laughed, which she was sure would have gotten her into even more trouble.

Master Peyta gave Master Teslan a short bow, and said, "He's your student".

Master Teslan turned to Squint, and said, "Did you three have a party last night? It's time to get going, if we're going to get to see anything today. We'll go rouse Vayan and Beldon. You get ready and meet us downstairs at the entrance."

As he turned to leave, he said, "And be quick about it, you've wasted enough of the day."

At the entrance, Master Peyta suggested that they go to the dining hall. He looked pointedly at the three students and said, "We should be able to find something to eat, and we can discuss what to do for the *remainder* of the day."

In the dining hall, it was apparent they were not the only ones that had slept in. Even though breakfast was no longer being served, there was a line of people near the array of snacks being offered.

After making their way through the line and choosing from an amazing assortment of fruits, vegetables, nuts, rolls, and more, the group found an empty table, and sat down to eat and discuss their options.

Master Peyta explained that they would be free to do whatever they chose during daylight hours today and tomorrow. The third day and last full day of their visit would be spent at the academy, learning about the school and the city, and what they had to offer newly-graduating students.

However, in order to avoid the kinds of trouble that night-time in a big city can create, the academy would be providing the entertainment for all three evenings. All groups where expected back at the academy before sundown. Any visitor that did not make it back on time would be confined to their room for the remainder of the trip.

In addition to its many libraries, the city offered a huge selection of cathedrals, museums, theaters, parks, and monuments from which to choose. For lunch, they could choose one of the many city's offerings, or if they wanted to save their funds, they could return here and enjoy the lunch provided by the academy. Master Peyta assured them that the meal would be just as good as last night's dinner had been, if that was their preference.

As they began considering their options, it became clear that the two librarians had spent their morning discussing what to do and where to go for the day. The three students were eager to get started, and so agreed to follow the librarians' advice. If there was something one of them really wanted to see that wasn't on today's itinerary, they could include it in tomorrow's excursion.

They started, of course, with the academy's library. Master Peyta explained that the library was one of the largest in the world. Its collection of academic works was unrivaled. He pointed out the restricted area, but it was not much bigger than the one in Kenna.

After leaving the library, Master Peyta pointed out some of the more interesting spots on the campus. Next to the library was a bookstore. Unlike Mr. Johnson's little book stand in Kenna, this bookstore was as big as a library.

He pointed out the magic center building, with its famous murals painted by academy students. There was the campus recreation center. Over there was the stadium, built over fifty years ago for watching organized sports events. There were dormitories scattered throughout the campus, and there was even a small lake.

Squint had been concerned that last night's revelations would affect how Vayan and Beldon behaved toward her, but it was as if nothing had changed. Well, for her, nothing *had* changed, but it appeared that nothing had changed for the two boys, either.

The group spent the rest of the morning visiting two of the Melsta's more interesting libraries. Master Peyta was familiar with the city's libraries, as he visited them regularly, looking for ideas for the academy library, and so was able to give them a knowledgeable tour. Because the students had overslept, he chose the libraries that he felt had the most unusual offerings.

The first library, called the Library of Lights, had a gorgeous pattern of lightroofs throughout the upper level. Peyta told them that the original librarian had designed the roof. The librarian had a talent that allowed him to filter the sunlight to prevent sun damage to the books. However, the effect of the filter was temporary, and had to frequently be re-applied. After the death of the librarian, finding someone with this talent to protect the books was difficult. The latest had been a student at the academy, but he had recently gone home. It was possible they would have to find a way to cover the lightroofs, if they couldn't find someone with the talent soon.

The second library had the most beautiful sweeping staircase Squint had ever seen. The problem with the staircase, Peyta told them, was that it took up too much of the library's space. Consequently, the size of the collection was a bit limited.

At lunch time, they visited one of the many outdoor markets. Here they found stalls selling an amazing variety of items. They all chose gifts for family and friends back home, and picked up an assortment of food to take to Gendry Park, one of the largest parks in the world.

Here, they found a place to sit and eat near the magnificent Gendry Fountain. The huge fountain was in the center of a carefully tended garden of colorful and exotic plants. Being the end of midden, many of the plants were in full bloom, and the sight was spectacular.

After lunch, they spent several hours visiting the exotic animal exhibits, and then tried their hand at the famous Hedge Maze.

The hedges of the maze were over six feet tall and thickly grown, making it impossible to see over or through them. The park had personnel posted in strategic positions throughout the maze for those that got hopelessly lost and needed assistance negotiating their way out. After much back-tracking and laughter, they managed to navigate their way through without assistance.

By the time they finished, it was nearly dusk and they had to hurry to make it back to the academy by curfew.

During dinner, it was announced that there were a number of choices for the evening's entertainment. There would be a play in the theater, with several famous performers. In the concert hall, the newest music sensation, the Doyen's, would be performing. The stadium would provide the venue for a game of squares, in which several famous professional players would be competing, and both local and visiting students were welcome to participate.

The social center would also be open, where there would be board and card games available for those that chose a quieter diversion. Or, of course, the visitors were welcome to spend the evening in their rooms, if that was their choice.

After stating that they trusted the three students would behave themselves if they were left unsupervised, Masters Teslan and

Peyta announced that they would spend a quiet evening playing cards in the social center.

Squint and the two boys had a lengthy discussion about which of the available options sounded best. Getting to see the famous entertainers perform would be great, but they finally decided that they would go watch the game of squares.

It turned out that the stadium was large enough to allow two simultaneous games. The three chose seats that would allow them to watch both games, and settled in for a pleasant evening.

To accommodate the number of students who wished to play, a total of three games were played in each square. The professionals were split between the two squares. One square had one professional playing pin and one playing pillar. The other had two professional pins and one professional pillar.

Everyone was rooting for the students to win, and in five of the six games, it was a student pillar who was left standing.

So with five student winners, and five professionals playing, it was decided that a final game would be played—professionals against the winning students. With one student and one professional in each of the five squares, it made for an exciting game. As the game neared its end, there were two students and one professional pillar remaining, each in a separate square. With the student pin aiming for the professional pillar, and the professional pin having to choose between two student pillars, it was immensely exciting.

The professional managed to hit one of the students, and the stands erupted. Everyone was on their feet cheering on the students. Cries of "Take him down!" rang throughout the stadium. It took three more rounds, but in the end, the professional pillar back-stepped to avoid the box and stepped out of the square. Cheers thundered around the stadium.

The three friends remained seated as some people made their way out of the stadium, and others made their way down to the stadium floor to meet the professional players. Once the crush had eased, they made their way out of the stadium and headed for their rooms. It had been a busy and exciting day, and after a quick good night, they went directly to their separate rooms.

CHAPTER 13

When everyone met the next morning, they had a leisurely breakfast while they discussed what to do for the day.

There were so many exciting things to choose from. Master Peyta said that he would be reimbursed by the academy for the cost of whatever they chose to do, so they should not let expense influence their decision.

He told them there was one place in town that he had always wanted to visit, but had never had the time or money to do so. He said that the International Museum of Natural Arts was supposed to be an absolutely amazing place. Although the entrance fee was a bit pricey, the museum was one of the largest in the world, and was the only museum of its kind. It held exclusively "natural" art. Which meant art that was created exclusively by non-talented artists.

The rest of the group looked at each other and nodded. Master Teslan said that, if this was something Master Peyta wanted to do, then so did they. And since everyone was done eating, they decided to head to the museum now, and figure out how they wanted to spend the afternoon when they stopped for lunch.

Since the museum was near Gendry Park, they would buy food at one of the outdoor markets and find a place near the Gendry Fountain to sit and eat and discuss what to do for the rest of the day.

When they got to the museum, as Master Peyta was reaching for his purse to pay the entrance fee, the young lady greeted him by name.

"I recognize you from the academy library. These are some of the students visiting from Kenna, right?" Master Peyta nodded. "We've been told that we should waive the entrance fee for any of the

Kenna visitors and their escorts. You are welcome to spend as much time as you like today free of charge. Here are your tickets."

With a huge grin on his face, Master Peyta thanked the young lady and preceded the group into the museum. Once they were all in, he turned and quietly said, "That is a great relief. Although the academy would have reimbursed me for the entrance fee, it would have taken the last of my funds to pay it, and I'm not sure how long I would have had to wait to receive the reimbursement. Now the visit will be much more enjoyable, without that worry on my mind."

Squint knew, just by the fact that he had shared this information with all of them, that it had been weighing heavily on him. It was a pleasure to see him so excited. As she glanced at Vayan and Beldon, it was clear that they felt the same.

The room they had just entered was huge. There were alcoves and niches all around the room, and several hallways leading off in different directions.

In the center of the room was a massive fish tank. As they headed in that direction, they realized that nothing in the tank was moving. The tank was full of fish and plants, and when they got closer, they could see sand at the bottom, with plants throughout, and crabs and snails here and there, and yet nothing within the tank moved.

When they got close enough, Master Teslan read the plaque that had information about the exhibit. It stated that the tank had been created by setting sand in the bottom of the tank, and then filling the tank with a clear gel. After the gel had set, the artist had used a needle to infuse color into the tank to create the various plants and animals. How the artist had managed to get the color in just the right spots without leaving trails of color in the gel, and without leaving any trace of the needle, was absolutely amazing. The accuracy of the details of each plant and fish, along with the crabs, snails and other items in the tank, was incredible.

They wandered through the museum for hours. They saw an exhibit in a room labeled "The Murder Room". The room contained around fifty paintings, each painting done in marvelous detail. The paintings each held a theme that was light and airy. For example, one was a garden scene, with butterflies and bees flying around beautiful flowers. Another was a forest scene, with lizards and big cats lounging about in the trees. And yet another was a beach scene, with birds and crabs playing in the tide.

Each painting was done with such incredible attention to detail that they looked just as good from a foot away as they did from five feet away. Squint was the first to notice that each painting had one jarring detail. Somewhere in each painting, painted in exquisite detail, was a murdered human body.

In the garden scene, on the back of one of the butterflies, there was a tiny female, sprawled on her back with a knife in her chest, and blood running from her chest to the back of the butterfly.

In the forest scene, over the head of a lizard, a miniature man hung from a noose, his head at an odd angle.

In the beach scene, far off in a corner, a miniscule woman lay face-down at the edge of the water, an arrow sticking up from her back, the foam from the tide slightly pink with her blood.

They ended up in a competition to see who would be the first to find the victim in each painting. They would all stand in front of a painting. As soon as someone spotted the body, they would step back from the painting, until all five had stepped back. When they finished, Beldon had spotted the body first the most often. They all agreed that the competition has been a bit macabre, but a lot of fun.

One room had a huge table in the center that contained a miniature town carved entirely from soap. The scene was complete with buildings, people, dogs and cats, bicycles, trees and bushes, and anything else you would find in a small town.

There was a box at the entrance to the room that contained magnifying glasses so visitors could view the amazing detail of the tiny pieces.

The scene included such detail that, with a magnifying glass, you could actually see the address and stamp on the envelope a woman was putting in the mailbox. You could see the label on the box of candy a man was handing a child, and the happy look the child had on his face.

The soap had been shaved so thin for the windows of the buildings that you could see details inside the various buildings. In the cafe, you could see people seated inside, with meat and vegetables on their plates, and steam coming from cups of something hot on the table. In one building, you could see people sitting at desks, and others that appeared to be walking around in the room.

When she looked really carefully, Squint even found a puppy relieving himself on a cherry tree in the town square. She laughed out loud when she noticed this detail, and everyone else joined her in laughter when she pointed out what she found so amusing.

Much later, as the group started down yet another of the many hallways, Beldon stopped dead in his tracks.

"Wait!" he said loudly. He looked around sheepishly and, said, a little quieter, "I know we haven't seen everything in the museum yet, but isn't anyone else hungry? Breakfast seems to have been forever ago!"

Once Beldon pointed it out, the rest of the group realized that they, too, were hungry, and agreed that it was probably time to go.

Since everyone appeared disappointed at having to leave, Squint pointed out that it was already mid-afternoon, and by the time they ate lunch, there would only be a few hours left before they had to be back at the academy. She suggested that they ask if their museum tickets would still be good if they left and came back. If they were, they could return and enjoy more of the museum after they ate.

Everyone agreed that this was an excellent idea. As they left, the same young lady who had given them their tickets this morning was at the door, and she said that the tickets she had given them were good until the museum closed that evening. They just needed to present them at the door when they returned.

CHAPTER 14

The group happily headed for the nearest open-air market to choose their lunch. They were chatting about what they had seen and marveling about the incredible detail in the various exhibits. Master Peyta reminded them that all of the exhibits had been created by artists with no magical talents, making the achievements even more remarkable.

As they wandered the market looking for souvenirs and deciding what to eat, Squint became aware of someone "probing" her mind very aggressively. Whoever it was would probe for a moment, back off, and then return a few minutes later. The probe was more than the normal probes she always felt in public places. It felt like it was directed at her, specifically. She continued to chat with the others, while trying to keep her mind block up in such a way that it appeared natural.

As they continued through the market, she was becoming concerned by the persistence of the probe, and worried about her ability to keep up her block without giving herself away. She kept touching her birthday stone for reassurance as they wandered the stalls.

When they had finished shopping and chosen their food, they began working their way out of the market towards Gendry Park. Vayan bumped into a man standing by one of the stands, nearly knocking him off his feet. The instant Vayan hit the man, the probe Squint had been trying to avoid abruptly ceased.

As Vayan was apologizing profusely to the man, Squint discreetly studied the man. He appeared to be in his mid-thirties. He was not a particularly large man, but was quite handsome, and looked very fit. It seemed as though only half his attention was on what Vayan was saying to him, and Squint believed that he was trying to "find" her again.

Not only was it obvious that this man had been the one probing her mind, but, for some reason, Squint was absolutely certain that this man was the Magician, and that he suspected he had been probing the mind of the Receptacle. She could only hope that her disguise would hold up, and he wouldn't realize she was a female masquerading as a male. If he discovered that, it would be the end of her for sure.

The two librarians and Beldon were looking at the man uneasily, as if they were a bit frightened by him. By the way Vayan was profusely apologizing, it was apparent that he, too, felt something disturbing about the man.

Master Teslan touched Vayan on the elbow, and said, "Come along, young man. We need to move on, or we're going to run out of time."

Gripping Vayan's elbow, he nodded to the man and quickly led the group out of the market. Squint was pretty sure the librarian had deliberately avoided using Vayan's name.

As they sat in the park eating lunch, Squint was quietly considering all the ramifications of the encounter with the Magician at the market. She was now positive that he was aware of the existence of the Receptacle, and was actively searching for her. She figured that his position in a busy spot of the market had kept him distracted and kept his probes intermittent, which had kept him from pinpointing the person he was probing.

She was very glad that the museum had been so interesting. It meant that her two friends' thoughts had still been focused on their experiences at the museum, leaving no room for thoughts about Squint's identity. She had no idea if the Magician had probed the two, but she assumed that he had been probing random people in search of information about the Receptacle. It wasn't beyond the realm of possibility that one, or both, of them had been probed.

Because he hadn't appeared to be a seller at the market, she had no idea whether the Magician lived in Melsta, or was just passing through. His clothing appeared to be of good quality, and was well cared for. His hair had been cut stylishly, and he was well-groomed. All of this together gave the impression that he was not short of funds, so he could very well have just been visiting the city.

Since she had already been working on keeping her secrets safe, the meeting wouldn't change her behavior much in that respect. She decided that she might have to work a bit harder on her mind block, but the encounter shouldn't affect her life too greatly.

It would have been nice to have a name to go with the face she could now recognize, but getting away from the market without being discovered was enough for her. She opted for enjoying the rest of her stay in Melsta without letting the encounter with the Magician ruin things for her.

The five spent what was left of the afternoon enjoying more of the museum's exhibits. Although Squint had decided not to let their meeting with the Magician ruin her visit, she found herself distracted by the thought of another chance encounter.

It seemed that her concern was affecting her enjoyment enough that the two boys were aware something was bothering her. At one point, Beldon quietly asked her what was wrong. She told him she would explain later, and he left it at that, but throughout the rest of the afternoon, she noticed both boys frequently glancing at her with concern.

They returned to the academy at dusk, and enjoyed another wonderful meal. During dinner, the headmaster of the academy announced that this evening's entertainment would be held in the Great Hall. The students of the academy would be presenting a talent show for their guests' enjoyment. It would include singing, dancing, comedy and drama. Everyone was invited. If they chose not to attend the performance, they were, of course, still welcome to avail themselves of the amenities in the social center, or to retire to their rooms.

In keeping with her decision not to let her encounter with the Magician ruin her visit, Squint suggested that they attend the performance. The two librarians, not surprisingly, said they would prefer the quiet of the social center. After looking at Squint questioningly, and getting a grin in return, Vayan and Beldon shrugged and agreed that the talent show sounded fun. The three said good night to the librarians and headed for the Great Hall.

Although most of the performances seemed to be very entertaining, she was still concerned about the encounter with the Magician. Or, rather, she was concerned about what to tell her two friends about it.

Since the remainder of the trip would be spent at the academy, the only chance of meeting the Magician again would be during their walk to the train station. However, as slight as that possibility was, it was still a possibility.

Her concern was, if she shared what had happened with Vayan and Beldon, and they did come across the Magician, would the Magician be able to "read" that information? She knew neither of her friends would give her away deliberately, but she also knew how difficult it was to keep yourself from thinking about something that you were trying not to think about.

However, while Vayan was apologizing to the Magician, the Magician appeared to be "searching" for the person he had been probing. He apparently had not been able to pinpoint her as the person he was probing. If that was true, then it was likely, even if they did encounter the Magician, he would be uninterested in them.

She finally decided she didn't care. The odds of them seeing the Magician again were very small, and she was tired of keeping secrets. When the show was over, she would tell Vayan and Beldon what had happened at the market.

Once she made that decision, she was able to sit back and enjoy the show. And enjoy it, she did. There were one or two acts that were a bit boring, but for the most part they were excellent. One juggling act was so bad, it was making people laugh. It wasn't until near the end of the act, when the juggler began doing amazing things with his juggling, that the audience realized he had been juggling poorly on purpose to make them laugh.

After the show was over, the three went to the dining hall to see if they could find some snacks. Even as late as it was, there was a nice choice of goodies. After they made their selections, Squint led them to a table at the back of the room, where they could talk without being overheard.

She quietly told them about the probe she had felt at the market, and her conclusion about the man that Vayan had almost knocked over.

Both boys clearly remembered the man, because of the way he had made them feel. Not fear, exactly. Just a feeling that something was not quite right.

All three agreed that this was almost certainly the Magician and they would need to keep an eye out for him in the future.

When they said goodnight outside their rooms, Vayan touched Squint on the shoulder.

"Thanks for trusting us enough to share your concerns about the Magician," he said. "I know it must have been hard, knowing that he might probe one of us and find out."

"You're my friends,' she said. "Besides," she said, grinning, "if he finds out, you'll be there to beat him up for me, right?"

And with that, they laughed and went to bed.

CHAPTER 15

The trip home was uneventful. Unlike the leisurely trip to get to Melsta, the trip home was accomplished quickly. They left Melsta first thing in the morning, and when they got to Rayne, they went directly from the ferry to the train for Kenna, which pleased Squint immensely.

They arrived at the Kenna station late in the evening. Although Beldon had the farthest to go, he had the least to carry, since he had arranged for most of his gifts to be sent to his family from Melsta. Vayan had filled his second suitcase to the brim with gifts for friends and family, and Squint had bought nearly as much for her grandmother.

The three students lingered long enough to thank Master Teslan for showing them such a great time. He said that he had enjoyed it very much, and was glad they had chosen to spend their time with an old man. After assuring him that they had thoroughly enjoyed his company, the three headed for their homes.

When she got home, Squint and her grandmother sat at the kitchen table, with the suitcase full of gifts on the table between them.

The first gift, which was covering all the other gifts in the case, was a robe much like the one Squint had received from the Rayne Academy. It was thick and warm, and had a cowl, just like the one from Rayne. The only difference was the color. Unlike the blue and silver of the Rayne robe, the one Squint bought her grandmother was a beautiful deep rose color.

The next gift in the case was a "special occasion" dress. It was also rose in color, was full length, with a wide, flowing skirt, and had hand-made lace at the throat and wrists.

Squint had found a stall at one of the markets that sold cookware, and had purchased several useful items for their kitchen.

She had also found a place that sold soap carvings. Although they weren't as well done as the ones at the International Museum of Natural Arts, they were still quite amazing. She had bought her grandmother a carving of a little girl sitting on a log reading a book that was quite detailed and absolutely adorable.

There were many other gifts, some practical, some fun, and her grandmother loved them all.

Squint had planned on telling her grandmother about having revealed her secrets to her friends, and about their encounter with the Magician, but by the time they had gone through all the gifts, it was late and her grandmother looked very tired. She decided it could wait until tomorrow.

The following morning was Saturday, and Squint's grandmother slept late. It was the first time Squint had ever known her to do so. When she finally got up, she still appeared tired, and was rather pale. Squint asked her if she felt okay, and her grandmother said she was afraid she might be coming down with something.

"But," she said, "I'm sure I'll be fine. And nowhere, in all those gifts you brought me, was there any food. We need to head into Kenna for some shopping, or we'll be going hungry next week.'

"There was something I wanted to talk to you about," said Squint, "but I guess it can wait until we get back from town."

However, by the time they got back from town, her grandmother looked terrible. Squint suggested that she go immediately to bed, and her grandmother agreed that this might be best.

Later than evening, Squint made some soup for her grandmother. When she took it into her grandmother's room, she found her grandmother sleeping, and decided not to wake her.

Her grandmother was still not feeling well the next morning, and spent the entire day in her room. At her grandmother's request, Squint went to the academy cafeteria to let them know her grandmother was ill and would not be there.

When she got to the cafeteria, the staff members appeared to be in a panic. "Squint, where on earth is Mrs. Nylls? We need to get things started right away, if they're going to be done on time." She wasn't sure why they were in such a panic. Her grandmother was retiring at the end of the midden term, so she had been training Miller, her first assistant to be the head cook. He should be able to handle things without her grandmother by now.

Squint explained that her grandmother was ill and would not be there today. Miller took a deep breath, and seemed to collect himself. "Oh, dear," he said. "Mrs. Nylls has never missed a day before. I hope she's feeling better soon. You tell your grandmother that we'll be fine, and she's to take as much time as she needs to get better," he said.

For the rest of the day, Squint let her grandmother sleep as much as she wanted. She made sure her grandmother had plenty of water, but mostly, she just left her alone. Around mid-day, she took her some soup. Her grandmother managed to eat a few bites, but went right back to sleep when she was done.

When it was time to leave for the academy the following morning, Squint's grandmother still wasn't up. Squint decided to leave her sleeping, and stop by the cafeteria to let them know she wouldn't be there.

When she got there, Miller and the rest of the staff were very concerned. Miller expressed his worry, but told Squint to assure Mrs. Nylls that he and the staff would follow her plans to the letter, so she shouldn't worry about anything except getting better. At Squint's questioning look, he explained that Mrs. Nylls always planned the academy meals a week in advance, allowing the staff to be well-prepared and comfortable with the menu. He said that, since she had begun training him, she had included him in creating these plans, so there should be no problems.

Squint had trouble paying attention during her morning classes, so at lunchtime, she decided she would go home to check on her Grandmother and see how she was feeling. She knew that Vayan and Beldon were likely to stop by the kitchen, so she would stop by on her way home and ask the staff to let the two know that her grandmother was ill.

As it turned out, she met the two boys just outside the kitchen, and explained that her grandmother was ill. She told them she was on her way home to check on her, and the two insisted on coming with her.

When they got to the Nylls home, they found Mrs. Nylls up and dressed. She was sitting at the kitchen table with some of Squint's soup and a cup of tea. She assured the three that she was feeling better, and should be ready to go back to work tomorrow. Squint didn't think she looked much better, but figured her grandmother knew best.

After a short visit, the three headed back to the academy. On the way, Vayan said, "Hey, did you tell your gramma that we know your secret yet?"

"No," said Squint. "I thought I'd wait until she was feeling better. Maybe you guys can come by tonight, and we'll tell her then. After we tell her, we can go to the magic training center, and you guys can help me train. We can work on Beldon's talent, too."

"I assume you have a talent that'll get us in without getting caught?" asked Beldon.

"Oh, yes," grinned Squint, "and I think you're going to like it. Let's meet at my house at the end of the day."

Knowing her grandmother was improving, Squint was able to pay more attention to her afternoon classes. After she finished her last class, she headed straight for home. When she arrived, she found Vayan and Beldon already there. She gave her grandmother a hug while she worked out how best to tell her about sharing her secrets with her friends.

She took a deep breath and started to speak, when there was a knock at the door. Annoyed at the interruption, Squint went to see who was at the door. Master McGillin, the academy headmaster, greeted her with a nod.

He said, "I heard that your grandmother was ill, and I came to see if there was anything I could do for the two of you. I have a minor healing talent, and thought I might be able aid in her recovery. I also wanted to see if there is anything you need while she is recovering."

Squint stepped back and invited him inside. On seeing the two boys, he said, "Good afternoon, Mister Dorn, Mister Heslan." He looked at Beldon, and said, "I understand that it's soon to be Master Heslan. Congratulations, I shall look forward to working with you. And I understand you are to join your father's business, Mister Dorn?" he asked Vayan.

"Yes, Sir. I'll start right after I finish at the academy," Vayan told him.

Master McGillin nodded at Vayan and said, "No vacation before you start?"

"No, I want to get right into it," said Vayan.

Master McGillin nodded again. "That sounds like a sensible plan," he said.

He turned to Squint's grandmother and said, "I'm very glad to see you up and about, Cayrah. You must be feeling better. I've been very worried about you, but I wasn't able to get here any earlier. I apologize for the delay."

"I appreciate your concern, Gerran, but there was no need for you to take time out of your busy schedule. I'm feeling better, and I'm sure I'll be back to work tomorrow."

"I was more concerned about you, than about your kitchen, Cayrah," Master McGillin said sternly. He smiled and said, "Here, let me take your hand and send a little healing your way."

Squint, who had been sitting next to her grandmother on the couch, moved so he could sit and touch her grandmother. Squint, who hadn't met anyone with the healing talent, wanted to see what he did.

She watched carefully as the headmaster took her grandmother's hand, bowed his head and concentrated for a short time. When he raised his head, he looked a bit drained. Her grandmother sighed and said, "I guess I didn't realize how poorly I still felt. I feel much better. Thank you, Gerran."

He didn't let go of her hands immediately. Instead, he looked closely at her and said, "You should have sent for me as soon as you began feeling poorly. You would not have ended up so ill you had to stay in bed and give everyone a scare."

She reached up and patted him on the cheek. "You're just worried about your dinner. You don't need to be concerned. Miller and the rest of the staff are well trained, and your dinner will be up to your exacting standards."

The headmaster smiled at her, and said, "You know me too well." He then looked at her seriously and said, "You continue to rest, and if you are not feeling perfectly well tomorrow, stay home and get better."

He glanced at Squint and said, "Squint, I'm counting on you to make her stay home, if she needs more rest. Either way, Cayrah," he said, "I'll come by first thing in the morning and give you another healing, just to be sure."

With that, he rose, nodded to Vayan and Beldon, smiled at Squint and her grandmother, and left the house.

As soon as she shut the door behind Master McGillin, Squint excitedly turned to her grandmother and said, "Gramma, why haven't we ever thought about a healing talent? I should be able to learn that, don't you think?"

She was briefly confused by her grandmother's look of dismay, until she realized that she still hadn't told her grandmother that Vayan and Beldon knew about her talents.

She glanced at the boys and went to sit beside her grandmother. She took her hands, and said, "I wanted to tell you when I first got home, but there were presents, and then you were ill, and it kind of got pushed aside," she said. "While we were in Melsta, I told Vayan and Beldon about my talents," she said. "I also told them that I'm a girl."

Her grandmother looked at her silently for a moment. She glanced at the two boys, and said, "Well, I'm sure you had your reasons, Squint, and I trust your judgment."

"There is one more thing, Gramma. While we were there, we had an encounter with a man that I'm sure was the Magician."

"Oh, Squint, you must have been so frightened." Her grandmother pulled her close in a hug, and said, "I take it everything was all right?"

With frequent interruptions from the boys, Squint told her grandmother about the encounter at the market.

After she finished describing the incident at the market, Vayan said, "Hearing it described that way, I'm much more inclined to agree that the man in the market was probably the Magician," he said.

Beldon was nodding his head in agreement, "It does sound much more likely, now that I've heard you describe things so clearly."

"I just wish I knew if he lived in Melsta, or was just passing through. I'd be much more comfortable knowing he was staying there, where we weren't likely to meet," Squint said.

Hugging Squint tight, her grandmother said, "From the sounds of your encounter, I'd say that he's actively searching for you, Squint. I think you can assume that he is not staying in one place. All we can do is hope that he doesn't find you until you are ready to be found."

"Maybe," said Beldon, "he'll stay in Melsta for a while, trying to find you again. In the meantime, when do we get to go to the magic center? I can't wait to see how we get there."

Squint looked at her grandmother and said, "Maybe we should wait a few days, until Gramma's feeling better."

Her grandmother responded with, "Don't be silly, Squint. Master McGillin's healing helped me immensely. And besides, whether you're here or not makes no difference to how well I feel. You can go tonight, but not for long. It's already late, and I don't want your studies to suffer."

"Well, if you're sure," said Squint.

"Take the boys home when you're done, or they'll be here until all hours."

Both boys looked at Squint curiously. "You'll see," she said. "Ready?"

The three got up, and both boys started towards the door.

"Not that way," Squint said. She held out her hands and said, "I'm not positive I need to be touching you, but just to be safe, come take my hands."

While Mrs. Nylls looked on with a grin, each boy took one of Squint's hands.

And they were in the magic training center.

Beldon began to speak, and then realized that they were no longer in the Nylls home.

"Oh, wow. You were right, Squint. I do like your method of getting us in here." Beldon turned to Vayan and said, "I don't know about you, but I could get used to that kind of travel."

"It's a bit—disconcerting," said Vayan. "But I agree, what a timesaver." He looked at Squint, and asked, "can you go anywhere you want like that?"

"I have to be able to visualize where I want to be," she said, "so I assume I can only go places I've already been. If I used a picture as reference, things could have changed, and I don't want to end up inside a wall, or something. And, of course, I'd probably scare people to death if I just appeared beside them, so timing is important, too." She grinned.

"Okay, so here's what I want to do to start with," she said. "I maintain a shield around Gramma and I while we're here, so I don't end up hurting one of us. I'll see if I can maintain a third shield, so I can shield both of you while we're here. I'll need to learn to do it with as little energy as possible."

"Isn't that going to affect your ability to concentrate on your magic?" asked Beldon.

"It might," Squint said. "But it'll help me to work on it. When I confront the Magician, I'm going to need to be able to concentrate on what I'm doing, regardless of any distractions, so the practice will be good for me."

Vayan glanced at Beldon, and said, "When you confront the Magician, you'll need to be shielding us while we help you, so you better learn to do it well."

Concentrating on getting shields maintained around both boys, it took a minute for what Vayan said to sink in.

"Help me? You want to help me?"

Again glancing at Beldon, Vayan said, "We've talked about this a lot in the last few days. We decided we can't let you do this by yourself. We know the risks involved as well as you do, but we also know what'll happen if the Magician wins. We want to be there to help."

Squint dropped to the floor and put her head in her hands. When she looked up, her face was streaked with tears. "You have no idea how much that means to me," she said. "The worst part of this whole thing for me has always been that I would have to face the Magician alone."

She stood and grabbed their hands.

"Hey, you got the hang of the shield," said Beldon. "It feels like you're touching me through a heavy layer of leather or something."

"Me, too," said Vayan, with a huge grin. "Which means that, not only have you shielded both of us, but you maintained it while you were crying like a baby."

Squint scowled at him. She rose and gave them each a hug, and said, 'Let's get started."

For that first day, Squint concentrated on keeping shields on everyone, and throwing various elements at her friends. Her friends concentrated on trying to thwart her efforts by distracting her in any way possible. They danced and cavorted, and generally behaved like idiots, while doing their best to dodge her magic.

This actually worked extremely well for Squint's purposes. Their erratic behavior made it difficult to aim with any accuracy. To add to the challenge, she began trying to hit both boys with the same blast.

Finally, Vayan danced into Beldon and sent them both careening in different directions. Beldon smacked into Squint and sent her flying. Everyone ended up on the floor, laughing uncontrollably.

Squint decided they'd had enough practice for today, and suggested that she take the boys home.

At first light the next morning, Squint woke to a quiet knocking at the door. She grumpily adjusted her appearance and answered it. She found Beldon standing on the porch. He apologized for the early hour, but said he was concerned about Squint's grandmother and wanted to see how she was doing.

She let him in and opened her mouth to say something rude about boys with no brains, when there was another knock at the door. Glaring at Beldon, Squint stomped over and opened the door again. There she found Vayan, who took one look at Squint's face, and edged around her to enter the house. He echoed Beldon's concern about Mrs. Nylls' health, along with an almost identical apology for arriving so early.

By then, Squint's grandmother was up, and thanking the boys for their concern. Squint gave both boys a nasty look, and stomped off to her room.

Squint's grandmother assured the boys that she was feeling much better, and would be returning to work today. She said, "I assume neither of you bothered to eat before you came. If you give me a minute to get dressed, I'll make everyone something to eat before we get started on our day."

She then said, very loudly, "And I'm SURE Squint will be HAPPY to join us."

At that point, there was another knock on the door. Vayan opened the door and greeted Master McGillin, who had come to provide Mrs. Nylls with the promised healing. When he finished, she invited the headmaster to join them for breakfast.

"As much as I would enjoy staying, I have other things which need my attention. I will have to wait to enjoy your cooking until the staff breakfast is served."

He gave Mrs. Nylls a hug and said, "I am very glad that you are feeling better."

"Thanks to you, I am," she said.

Once he left, she persuaded the boys to help her with breakfast, while Squint finished getting ready.

After breakfast, the four walked to the campus together. Since neither of the boys had classes, Squint's grandmother suggested that they either join her in the kitchen, or go wait at the Nylls house for Squint to finish her day. Squint was quite sure she would find them getting fat in the kitchen at the end of the day.

Squint spent her lunch period at the library, rather than in the kitchen, so she didn't see Vayan and Beldon until she and her grandmother arrived home that evening. Despite her rather bad-tempered notion about finding them in the kitchen, the boys had found something to do with their day, and had only arrived at the house a short time before she and her grandmother.

Squint had her arms full of large books she had picked up at the library at lunchtime. She plopped them on the kitchen table, sorted through them, and handed four of them to Beldon.

"Here, these are for you. You'll need to share them with Vayan when you're done."

"Anatomy?" asked Beldon.

"Yes, I think knowing how your body works will help immensely in learning to control your talent," Squint said. "Be careful with those, I don't want to get in trouble for lending them to you."

She looked at Vayan and said, "I think that it might help you use less effort to control yours, Vayan, which would let you enhance your abilities for longer periods."

Beldon glanced curiously at the rest of the books on the table. "Oh, you'll get to those eventually," grinned Squint. "But for right now, they're for me. They're advanced anatomy and physiology."

She went to her grandmother and gave her a hug. "I want to be able to use the healing talent. But it seemed to tire Master McGillin pretty quickly. I want to see if I can do it without getting exhausted. If I know how the body works, maybe I can do that. If I can heal effectively, I'll have a much better chance at beating the Magician.

She looked at the two boys, and said "I'm also hoping you'll help me learn to do what the two of you do." Looking grim, she said, "When the time comes, I'm going to need every advantage I can get."

The three friends began spending four or five evenings a week at the magic center. Although Squint's grandmother would occasionally join them, she usually fed them and sent them on their way.

While Squint normally had a full day of classes, Vayan and Beldon only had a few classes to finish up before they graduated. The two spent most of their time together, working on their respective talents. Well, mostly honing Beldon's talent.

The two boys took a cursory glance at the books Squint had brought them, and then decided to do things their own way.

Beldon's biggest problem with using his talent was being able to increase or decrease just one of his senses. He was able to dampen or enhance all of his senses at once. He was getting better at enhancing one sense while completely dampening all others. But he was unable to heighten one sense while leaving the others unchanged. He wanted to be able to completely control which senses he changed.

Depending on which sense was to be the focus, they would spend their day on the beach east of Kenna or in the woods south of campus.

If it was the beach, Vayan would run as far as he could, and Beldon would keep track of his movements with enhanced vision, while attempting to maintain a normal level with his other senses. In the beginning, Vayan would hardly break a sweat before Beldon lost sight of him, but as the season progressed, it became a competition to see which came first, Beldon losing sight of Vayan, or Vayan running out of energy.

This soon became rather boring, and the boys relegated it to the days that were exceptionally hot, so they could play in the water after a run or two.

If Beldon was focusing on sound or smell, they would go to the woods.

When they worked on his sense of smell, Beldon would dampen all his senses, and Vayan would take a circuitous route through the woods. He would leave small clues to his route by bending twigs or scratching bark on trees. He would work his way back to Beldon, who would then attempt to track the route by following Vayan's scent, trying to maintain his other senses while enhancing his sense of smell.

When the sense was sound, Beldon would dampen all his senses. Vayan would run through the woods as quickly as possible. After a short time, Beldon would shout that he was ready, and Vayan would then slow down and begin randomly changing his route, being as quiet as possible. Beldon would try to locate Vayan using only his enhanced hearing.

This activity led to the discovery that Vayan could use his talent to control his muscles in such a way as to allow him to move much more quietly. He found that this actually took more effort than maintaining energy while he ran.

As midden went on, and they both improved their skills, this became their favorite of the three activities. Since Vayan had the advantage of being at a distance, it was often dark before Beldon found Vayan, and then it was usually because Vayan walked into something he couldn't see, giving away his position.

Beldon eventually decided—totally in the interest of improving his talent, of course—to try enhancing two of his senses at once, while keeping the others at their normal level. He added vision to hearing, and was able to track Vayan in no time at all.

It didn't take Vayan long to realize Beldon was cheating, and for both boys to realize they were getting bored with the games.

They decided to talk to Squint to see if they could substitute some of the time they were spending in the magic center with outside activities. With two people to track, Beldon would have more trouble finding them. With two people to trick, Vayan would have to be even quieter. And it would allow Squint to work on her own enhancement talents.

The three of them spent the remainder of midden learning as much as they could about their various talents.

CHAPTER 16

In addition to her studies and talent training, Squint spent time with her grandmother discussing what Squint was going to do at the end of midden. Even though Squint was only fifteen, the faculty at the school believed her to be seventeen, with one year of study before graduation. However, because she had "completed" many classes before she actually became a student, the only area in which Squint hadn't completed studies was high magics, involving runes and rituals. Although she had an interest in this field, neither she and nor her grandmother believed it would offer any help in defeating the Magician.

So, although she wouldn't officially graduate, both Squint and her grandmother agreed Squint would be finished with the academy at the end of the midden term. But then what?

Squint felt she needed to travel. She suspected there were talents she had yet to discover that would help her in her quest to defeat the Magician. She believed that she had learned all she could from the academy, and needed to broaden her learning by meeting new people. Squint's idea was for the two of them to travel to various places, and see what new talents Squint could uncover.

Mrs. Nylls felt that was a rather haphazard way to go about things. Her suggestion was for Squint to spend time doing research on various talents and how they might help in her upcoming battle. Once she discovered talents that could help, she could work to master them. This was something that could be done right here, without traveling, and taking a chance on the Magician discovering her whereabouts prematurely.

As midden moved on, Squint's grandmother began spending less time at the cafeteria. She frequently slept late, and even took days off during the week. She said she wanted Miller to get used to handling things without her around, but Squint suspected that she really just enjoyed the free time.

Just two weeks before the end of the term, Squint came home to an empty house. After searching the entire house, she moved outside to check the yard. She found her grandmother on the ground behind the house. She was unconscious and barely breathing. Although her grandmother was not a small woman, Squint picked her up and carried her to her bed. She covered her, and took her hand in an attempt to ascertain what was wrong. She was so upset, she couldn't remember what to do. She traveled to the hallway outside Master McGillin's room and knocked loudly on his door.

When he answered the door, she frantically explained what had happened, and asked him to come help her grandmother. Master McGillin quickly put on a robe and followed Squint to her grandmother's room. Once there, he said he wanted to see Cayrah alone, and shut Squint outside the room.

After what seemed an eternity to Squint, but was actually a very short time, the door opened, and Master McGillin came out and shut the door behind him. As Squint started to speak, he reached out and touched her arm.

"Let's go sit down," he said.

After looking back at her grandmother's door, Squint went to the couch and sat down. Master McGillin sat beside her and took both her hands in his.

'I don't know how to say this, Squint." He took a deep breath and sighed. "Your grandmother is gone," he said, and bowed his head.

Squint just sat and looked at Master McGillin like he had spoken in a foreign language. What he said made no sense. What did he mean, her grandmother was gone. Gone where? When was she coming back? Why did she go without saying anything to Squint?

After a short time without a response from Squint, Master McGillin raised his head and asked her, "Do you understand what I'm telling you Squint? You're grandmother has died."

"Well, of course she hasn't," Squint replied sharply. "She'll be just fine. I came and got you so you could heal her. She's going to be just fine."

"Squint, I'm sorry, but she was gone by the time I got here. There was nothing I could do for her."

"Oh, don't be silly," Squint said. She was crying, and didn't even realize it. "She'll be fine. Just fine. She'll get up, and everything will be just like always."

The headmaster reached out and gently took Squint into his arms. There was nothing left to say. He held Squint until she had cried herself to sleep. He rose quietly, and left Squint on the couch. He was reluctant to leave her alone, but there were things that needed to be done.

Since Squint was Mrs. Nylls' only relative, there was no one to be notified, and Master McGillin, thankfully, took care of the arrangements for the ceremony. This left Squint with nothing to do but wait. She spent the days between her grandmother's death and her day of flames in a fog. It was as if this was all happening to someone else, and she was standing beside this other person watching. Beldon and Vayan remained by her side, but she seemed unable to gain any comfort from their presence.

The day of flames for Cayrah Nylls was attended by nearly everyone at the academy and a great many people from Kenna. It was amazing how many people mourned the loss of Squint's grandmother. Beldon and Vayan stood close to her on either side, each holding a hand and doing their best to give her their support and comfort.

Once the ceremony was over, Beldon and Vayan walked Squint home. After her initial tears the night of her grandmother's death, Squint had not cried. When she arrived home to an empty house, and finally realized that she would never see her grandmother again, Squint was overwhelmed by tears. Her best friends sat close on either side of her, each holding a hand, and waited while Squint mourned.

Finally, she straightened and gave each of her friends a hug.

"You have no idea how much having you two by my side has meant to me," she said. "Without you, I would be totally alone in this world, and I can think of nothing worse. Now I need some time to figure out what I'm going to do. Give me a day or two, and then we can get back to training."

Both boys gave her a hug and left. She felt bad about lying to them, but felt it was for the best. She knew they would not be getting back to training, because she would be leaving tomorrow.

She would leave a note for Beldon and Vayan, explaining what her plans were. She would be able to travel home occasionally, but she needed to get out in the world and learn. She also needed to get away from this house and its memories for a while.

She didn't tell her friends what she was planning because she was afraid they would consider her too young to be traveling alone, and would attempt to prevent her from leaving. If she was a normal seventeen-year-old girl, she would consider herself too young, too. But she was a very unusual fifteen-year-old girl, with enough talents to keep her safe while she was traveling. At least that's what she hoped.

Being honest with herself, she didn't want to say goodbye to her friends in person because she was afraid that, being the good friends they were, they might be able to convince her that she should stay.

She would stop by the administration office tomorrow and tell them what her plans were. Believing that she was a seventeen-year-old male, no one should have an issue with her leaving. Once they were notified, she would head out.

She spent several hours composing notes for her best friends, explaining what she was doing, and why she had chosen to let them know by note, rather than in person.

In the morning, Squint packed a small satchel with some clothing and other things she thought she might need, and headed for the administration building. Headmaster McGillin wasn't available, which was actually a bit of a relief for Squint, so she spoke with the assistant headmaster and informed him that she would no longer be attending the academy. He discussed her academic achievements with her, and then said that it sounded like she had made the right decision.

He offered to take care of all the appropriate paperwork, and she said she appreciated it. She did not tell him that it might be more difficult than he was anticipating, since she had never been officially enrolled at the academy.

She also decided that there were two more stops that she needed to make before she left the area.

She went to the library and shared a tearful goodbye with Master Teslan. He said he was sorry to see her go, but understood why she felt it necessary. He asked that she come back to visit him as often as she could manage.

Her second stop was Kenna, where she visited Mr. Johnson at his book shop. After another tearful goodbye, Squint hoisted her satchel and set off.

CHAPTER 17

Squint decided to follow the coast north. There wasn't much south of Kenna and the academy, and she had already traveled west when she visited Melsta. Traveling north would take her through her hometown of Eslan, and then Ander, Sella and Greyn, until she reached Norla, on the northern coast. She imagined that by the time she reach Norla, she would be ready for some time at home, and she could decide then where to go next.

Having a father who was a hunter, and a mother with an interest in herbalism, Squint felt that she should have no problem fending for herself while on the road. When she found farms or arrived in towns, she could work in exchange for food and a place to sleep.

She had done a lot of thinking during midden about where she would go and what she would do, if she left the academy. It was important that she appear normal and not do anything that would attract the attention of the Magician. This meant keeping her use of talents to a minimum. She felt the best way to do this, while continuing to hone her many talents, would be to select one or two talents and focus on those, presenting them as her only talents.

She would stay in an area for a while, and then travel on to a new area and choose a different talent. If it seemed necessary, she could alter her appearance as she traveled, so that no one became aware that she had more talents than she should. This method should prevent unwanted attention, while still allowing her to work on multiple talents.

After leaving Kenna, she continued north along the road toward Eslan. Just before arriving at Eslan, she veered off the road and headed slightly west, toward her old home. As she topped the hill where she had stopped and watched her house burn nine years ago, she stopped again. Looking down, there was nothing to show that her home had ever been there. This made her sad, but also pleased her that she had been able to thwart Mr. Bronday's desire to own her home.

When Squint was young, and had become aware of her talents, she realized that it was a talent that had warned her that something was wrong while she was on the beach the afternoon her family died. She also realized that her anger that day had triggered another talent, which had set the fierce blaze that had consumed her home.

She still remembered very little about the trip to her grandmother's home. When she had arrived at her grandmother's, she told her grandmother that Mr. Bronday had killed her family, and had burned her house down. She remembered her grandmother sending someone from the academy to check on the story.

She never understood why Mr. Bronday wasn't punished for killing her family. She and her grandmother never discussed it, but she assumed there was a good reason it hadn't been pursued. She had planned on asking her grandmother about it someday, but now it was too late.

Deciding not to go any closer to the spot where her home used to be, she turned to the east and returned to the road, to continue her journey.

She traveled for nearly a week before reaching Ander. She met very few people on the road, and traveled at a slow pace, enjoying the weather. She did practice her talents a bit, but spent most of the time with her own thoughts, missing her grandmother and her two best friends.

Ander was about the same size as Kenna. When she arrived, the first thing Squint looked for was the library or book seller. In most small towns, the library or book seller was a central place, and often contained a bulletin board on which people posted information about things for sale, available jobs and rooms for rent.

Even if there wasn't a bulletin board, the librarian or book seller would be a good source of information about the town. In Kenna, people were always stopping by to talk to Mr. Johnson and let him know what was going on in town.

She found the book seller where she expected, right in the heart of town. There was a young lady seated behind the stand, reading a huge book. As Squint approached, she looked up grinned.

"I haven't seen you before," she said. "I'm kind of new here, and haven't met everyone yet," she continued. "My name is Marmie, and I moved in with my Uncle Terr last month. He lets me watch the bookstand sometimes, when he has things to do."

"Nice to meet you," said Squint. "My name's Squint, and you haven't seen me before because I just got here," she said. "I'm hoping to find a job and a place to stay for a while."

"You're traveling by yourself? That sounds wonderful. If you have time, maybe you can tell me about your travels. I want to write a book someday, and I like hearing about things people have done and places they've been." She tilted her head and said, "Uncle Terr says it's just because I'm nosy, and I guess that's probably true." She grinned again.

Squint started to speak, but Marmie pointed and said, "There's Uncle Terr now. He'll be able to help you find what you want."

Squint turned to see a stout, dark-haired man coming their way, carrying a bag filled with what appeared to be vegetables. As he neared, he smiled at Squint and reached out with his empty hand.

"Hi, I'm Terr Fost, bookseller here in Ander." He gripped Squint's hand and said, "So what brings a young man like yourself to our lovely town?"

"I was just traveling through," said Squint, "but I thought I might stay for a while. Maybe work for a bit, and save up some money for my travels."

"Where're you coming from, if you don't mind my asking?"

"I was a student at the Kenna Academy." With a sigh, Squint said "My grandmother recently died, so I've decided to travel and see some of the world."

Marmie squealed, and said, "You were at the academy? Wow, you must be really smart. I wanted to go, but I'm a girl. Was it wonderful? How long were you there? What was your favorite class? Who was your favorite teacher?"

Smiling fondly at Marmie, Terr Fost said, "Whoa, slow down girl. "He wouldn't have time to answer your questions, even if he wanted to."

He turned to Squint. "Let's start by getting you a place to stay, and seeing what kind of work you're interested in. Do you have enough money to pay for a place, or will you need some assistance with that?"

"Oh, no," Squint said. I have a bit that I saved up before I left home. I will need to find work soon, though. I was hoping you could help with that."

"I know of a good place for you to stay," said Mr. Fost. "Mrs. Gern has a small room for rent, and she doesn't ask much for it. She'll rent to you for next to nothing, if you're willing to help her with chores around the house. She lives just around the corner there."

"Marmie, will you watch the stand for a bit longer, while I walk young Squint here to Mrs. Gern's house? We can talk about work on the way, Squint."

"Okay,' Marmie replied. "Come back and tell me about your travels sometime, Squint," she said.

Squint had already decided that the talent that she needed to work on the most was her most recent—healing. She wanted to be able to do effective healing without completely draining her energy.

So when Mr. Fost asked what kind of work she was interested in, she said, "I have a small healing talent, and will be happy to offer my services to people," she said. "But I'm also willing to do whatever else I can to help people out."

Mrs. Gern was a tiny women. She appeared to be quite old, but was still fit. When Mr. Fost introduced Squint, she said, "Oh, I do hope you're looking for a room, young man. My stepstool broke, and I can't get to my dinner plates."

She laughed and said, "Let me show you the room I have, and you can decide if you like it. If you do, we can discuss price while you get down plates for our dinner."

Mr. Fost said, "I'll leave you to Mrs. Gern's care, then. Come see me first thing in the morning, and we'll see what we can do about getting some work for you."

Squint spent the next two months in Ander, honing her healing talent and earning plenty of money on odd jobs. Her services were constantly in demand, both because she worked hard and was good at what she did, and because people enjoyed her company.

As Mr. Fost had indicated, Mrs. Gern charged a minimal amount for the room, and included meals with the price. Squint, in turn, fixed all sorts of things in the house and yard, and even did some painting for Mrs. Gern.

Although she didn't have any travel stories, she enjoyed Marmie's company, and they spent quite a bit of time together, discussing everything under the sun. Squint had never had a female friend before, and wished that she could truly be herself while she was with Marmie.

Squint spent her spare time in the library, looking for any information about the final confrontation. Although *The Sacrifice of the Talents*, the book she found at the Kenna Academy library, had been in the restricted area, it had been because of the rarity of the book, not because the information it contained was restricted.

She found several books regarding the sacrifice of talents, the Receptacle and the Magician, and the final confrontation. The stories all varied somewhat in their description of the original sacrifice of talents and the circumstances of the final confrontation, but the basics were the same in all of them. Although the stories were interesting to read, none of them contained anything particularly helpful.

When she was out of things to fix for Mrs. Gern, she decided it was time to move on. On the eve of her departure, Mrs. Gern invited a number of Squint's new friends to what she called a "traveling on" party for Squint.

Having a party just for her was a new experience for Squint, and one that she thoroughly enjoyed. She was sad to be leaving here, where she had made so many new friends, but needed to move on to the next stage of her travels.

After everyone had gone home, and Mrs. Gern had gone to bed, Squint decided she wanted to visit her grandmother's house. Although she still sorely missed her grandmother, the initial grief had lessened, and she wanted to see how the house was faring.

Leaving her things in her room, she traveled to her old bedroom. She looked around, and was amazed to see an immaculately clean room. Where there should have been two month's worth of dust, there were only clean surfaces. She walked to the bed and picked up a pillow. It smelled freshly cleaned.

She turned to leave the room, and was immediately tackled and knocked to the ground. She reacted instantly, "threw" the tackler off her, and jumped to her feet.

As she started to use one of her talents to throw attacker to the ground, he shouted, "Squint, stop! It's me!"

She stayed her attack, and then realized it was a good thing she had, because her attacker was Beldon.

"What are you doing here," she demanded. "I could have really hurt you!"

"Settle down," Beldon said. "Let's go in the kitchen and talk."

Once they were settled at the table, tea in hand, Squint frowned and said, "Explain what you're doing here, Beldon."

"Waiting for you to show up," he said, with a frown of his own.

"How could you leave us with nothing but a note, Squint? We thought we were your friends."

"You *are* my friends, Beldon. That's why I left the note."

She reached across the table and took his hands. "I truly am sorry, Beldon, but I was afraid you would talk me out of leaving. I couldn't let that happen."

She brought her hands back across the table and again frowned at him. "But what are you doing here, Beldon, in my house? I'm assuming you've been here for a while, and have been keeping it clean?"

Seeing the frown on her face, he looked down at the table and said, "Since this isn't really much farther away from the classroom for me than walking from the dorms, and since I'm used to doing my own cleaning, Vayan and I decided I should just move in here and take care of things until you got back."

He looked up, saw the glare on her face, and looked back down at the table. "We assumed you would come back here at some point. We talked about it, and decided we wanted to confront you when you did. The only way to do that would be for someone to be here when you showed up."

"Okay, I'm here. So now what?" Squint asked.

"Well, it's not too late. Can we go get Vayan, and talk about this?"

A moment later, Squint was looking at Beldon with both hands over her mouth, trying to stifle her laughter.

They were in the woods, just past Vayan's house, and Beldon was sprawled on the ground. scowling up at her.

"You could have warned me," he said.

"I'm sorry," she said, still trying to stifle her laughter. "I guess I should have had you stand up before I brought us here."

It should have occurred to her that traveling from a sitting position without the chair he was sitting on would be a problem. When they arrived in the woods, he had still been sitting, but sitting on nothing.

Vayan's grandmother answered the door when they knocked.

"It's late, why are you here?" she barked at them.

"Can we see Vayan," Squint asked sweetly.

"I said it's late. Come back tomorrow," she said, and slammed the door in their faces.

They looked at each other in surprise. "Should we knock again?" Beldon asked.

As Squint started to respond, the door opened and Mrs. Dorn looked out.

"I am so sorry," she said. "She's a bit grouchy today." And then she realized who was on her doorstep. "Oh, Squint. It's wonderful to see you. The boys have missed you so much."

She reached forward, grabbed Squint's arm and dragged her into the house. "Come in, come in."

Beldon followed behind and shut the door.

"Vayan," shouted Mrs. Dorn, without letting go of Squint. "Come see who's here."

Vayan wandered in from the kitchen, spotted Squint and sprinted across the room. He gathered her in a tight hug, lifting her clear off the floor.

Once the initial greetings were over, Vayan told Mrs. Dorn that they were going to go to Squint's house to catch up. "Don't be too late Vayan. You need to be at the shop early tomorrow," she said.

As soon as they reached the woods, Squint used her talent to take them to her home.

"Hey!" Vayan glared at Squint as he caught his balance, barely keeping himself upright.

"Be glad you weren't sitting down," Beldon said. "Squint doesn't seem to think warnings are necessary. As you see, Vayan," said Beldon sardonically, "Squint has learned how to take you with her without touching you."

"I said I was sorry," Squint said with a grin. "I really will try to warn you next time."

They spent the remainder of the night catching up on things and discussing what should happen next.

After telling her two friends about her time in Ander, Squint told them that she was wishing it wasn't so dangerous for a female to travel alone. Otherwise, she would give up her disguise as a boy, and travel as herself.

Vayan told them he was unhappy with his situation. As much as he loved the work he was doing, he was having difficulty working with his father.

"I know there are things I still need to learn," he said," but the only work he allows me to do, a ten-year-old could handle. He let me do more while I was still in school than he does now." He shrugged. "I think it's time for me to move on."

"If I came with you Squint, you could pretend to be my sister, and travel as yourself."

Beldon was nodding his head. "I could travel with you, too."

"I thought you were happy teaching," said Squint.

"I never really thought about doing anything but teaching," he said. "It was just the natural thing to do after school. But I'm bored. To be quite honest, the only reason I'm still here is because I don't know what else to do with myself. Maybe if I travel with you, I can find something better."

She looked at the two for a moment. "Are you sure this is want you want? There won't be many options to come home, since disappearing from town every night is not practical. But having you two with me while I travel would be absolutely wonderful."

"Then it's settled," said Beldon. "First thing in the morning, Vayan can tell his parents, and I'll let Master McGillin know. There's no reason we can't leave right away."

With a serious look her friends, Squint said, "There is one more thing I need to tell you two before we go. I'm not even sure why I haven't told you before, but I want you to know everything there is to know about me."

The boys looked at each other, and then looked at Squint with curiosity. "I'm not sure what else there can be for you to tell us, but we're listening," said Vayan.

She took a deep breath, and then shared her last secret. "I had a birthday while I was on the road," she said.

Looking at Vayan, Beldon said, "Yes, we had a drink in your honor."

"It was my sixteenth birthday," she said.

"Sixteen! So you were traveling around by yourself at fifteen? Are you crazy?" Vayan was staring at her like she'd lost her mind.

Beldon turned to Vayan and said, "You do remember what he can do? I'm reasonably sure he was quite safe traveling alone."

"Oh, of course," Vayan said. "I forgot for a minute who I was talking to." He grinned at Squint.

"He," thought Squint. She wasn't sure how she felt about the fact that the two boys apparently still thought of her as a male. It meant that they were not likely to inadvertently give up her secret, but it also meant, with her grandmother gone, there was no one to think of her as Serran, rather than Squint.

At this point, the three realized the sun was rising. They had talked right through the night. Squint fixed them all some breakfast, and then the two boys went off to finalize their plans for departure.

CHAPTER 18

After very clearly warning them that they were going to travel, Squint had taken them to the spot just north of Ander from which she had traveled home. She asked them to wait for her while she picked up her belongings and said her final goodbyes in Ander.

Once she returned, the three friends headed north, towards Sella and Greyn, and then Norla, on the northern coast.

As much as Squint would like to drop her disguise and travel as a female, the three had decided that this was just not a good idea. Three young men traveling together is nothing special. Two young men traveling with a young girl could attract attention they didn't want. It was more sensible for her to maintain her disguise for the time being.

While they traveled, the two boys—well men, Squint thought—had talked a lot about what they wanted to do with their lives.

Vayan thoroughly enjoyed woodwork and building beautiful furniture, but working with his father was impossible. He had already decided that, if he wanted to make a living as a furniture maker, he was going to have to leave Kenna. He figured that traveling with Squint would give him an opportunity to find a good place.

Beldon, too, was unhappy with his situation, but for a different reason. He found himself in a position that was utterly boring to him. He admitted to his two friends that he had more or less drifted into the position of teaching. He had no idea what he wanted to do with his life, and had just followed the suggestion of his teachers. He now knew that it wasn't what he wanted to do with his life, but still had no idea what he wanted to do.

Vayan had a number of ridiculous suggestions. He suggested that Beldon would make a great clown. Or maybe he should play squares for a living. Then he suggested that, with his ability to hear people coming from far away, Beldon would make a great thief.

Squint suggested that he would make a good peace officer. Beldon said that he would just end up sitting around waiting for something to happen, which would be even worse than teaching.

Later, as they were talking about Squint's time in Ander, Squint was certain she'd thought of the perfect job for Beldon.

"I know what would be the perfect job for you, Beldon."

She skipped forward a few steps, and then turned around, walking backwards. She wanted to see Beldon's face when she told him what she was thinking.

'You should be a librarian!"

Vayan clapped his hands and, with a huge grin, said, "Brilliant! Absolutely brilliant!"

Beldon just continued walking. Squint couldn't tell whether he liked the idea or not. She moved next to him. Without looking at him, she said, "It was just an idea. It's fine if you don't like it."

Vayan, apparently oblivious to Beldon's lack of reaction, said, "What? What's not to like. He'd make a superb librarian."

Beldon just kept walking.

A bit disappointed in Beldon's reaction, Squint finally decided to change the subject, and they went on to talk of other things.

That night, after they found a spot to sleep, Squint was off from the campsite a bit, playing with some elemental magic. She could conjure fire, ice and wind, but was having a bit of trouble with water. For some reason, she could barely get a trickle.

Beldon wandered over to see what she was doing. She said she was trying to make it rain. Beldon laughed and said, "Well, if you're going to make it rain, make it rain on me. I stink."

As he finished speaking, Squint finally got the spell right, and a huge torrent of water splashed down.

Right on Beldon's head.

Several days later, as it was just becoming full dark, it started to rain lightly. Vayan noticed a light off to the east of the road. After a very short discussion, they all agreed they wanted to see if the light came from a place where they could offer their services in exchange for a night inside, and maybe some home-cooked food.

As they got closer, they could tell it was a house. When they neared the yard, a dog came rushing towards them, barking ferociously. Vayan backed away, saying, "Do something, Squint!"

Squint decided to see if her ability to calm an angry person extended to animals. She squatted down and used her talent to "touch" the dog's mind. Although the dog's mind was very different from a person's, she was able to sooth it, just as she would a person. It quit barking, and started wagging its tail. It trotted over to Squint and let her pet it.

As Squint rose, a woman came out of the house carrying a very large shotgun, pointed directly at Squint.

"What did you do to her," she shouted. "Get away from her."

Squint, hand still on the dog's head, said, "I'm sorry ma'am. Animals just seem to like me. I meant no harm."

"What do you want?" the woman demanded.

"My friends and I are traveling, and thought we'd stop and see if we could trade our services for a place to sleep for the night," Squint. "We're willing to do most anything you need."

The woman lowered the shotgun a bit, and said, "And how do I know I can trust you?"

Wiping rain from her face, Squint sighed, and said, "I'm sorry ma'am. We'll just move along and not bother you."

She patted the dog again, and said quietly, "Come on guys. A night under a roof in not worth upsetting her."

Squint turned to leave, and Vayan and Beldon joined her. As the three started to move away, the dog whined.

The woman said, "Wait. I guess if Cookie likes you, it's okay. I've never seen her take to someone like that before." She lowered the shotgun to her side and said, "Come on in."

Squint looked back and said, "It's okay. We don't want to make you uncomfortable."

"No, it's fine," the woman said. "I'm just not used to company."

Once they were inside, the woman provided towels so the three could dry off, and everyone took seats around the kitchen table. Cookie immediately settled next to Squint, leaning hard against her leg.

While the woman started a kettle of water for tea, and turned on the heat under a pot of soup that was sitting on the stove, she introduced herself as Satie Looj. She said her husband Jode was out hunting, and should be home soon. She said they would eat as soon as he arrived.

She explained that she was expecting her first child, and thought maybe that was why she was so nervous when they first appeared.

"Oh, no, we understand," said Beldon. "Three strangers showing up on your doorstep in the dark would make anyone nervous." He introduce everyone, and they all chatted comfortably until Jode got home.

When Jode arrived, he was carrying a shotgun identical to the one Satie had. He raised it menacingly, and then noticed Cookie, sitting so comfortably by Squint. Without dropping the shotgun, he looked questioningly at Satie, and she told him, "Cookie's taken a liking to him," and shrugged.

Once Jode was reassured, Satie introduced everyone, and told Jode that she had invited the three travelers to share dinner and spend the night. She asked Jode to fetch a chair from the porch, and served soup and fresh bread to everyone. Even Cookie got a small bowl of soup.

Jode said that he was afraid that there wasn't room for them in the house, but they were welcome to sleep in the barn, which was warm and dry. He said they didn't have any animals yet, so all it contained was bits of extra furniture.

Satie handed Squint a pile of blankets, and told them they were welcome to come in and have some breakfast in the morning, before they went on their way.

"Aren't there some chores that need doing before we leave?" asked Vayan. "We're used to working for what we get," he said.

"Like he'd been on the road for years, not days," Squint thought with a smile.

Satie looked at Jode, and he said, "We can talk about that over breakfast."

Morning brought with it a heavy rainstorm. Jode and Satie invited the three to stay until the storm was over, and they agreed, as long as there was something they could do to repay the Looj's for their hospitality.

It turned out there were enough chores to last them several days past the end of the storm. Jode spent his days hunting, and Squint had the suspicion that Satie was creating chores for them so she wouldn't have to be alone. They were enjoying the company and Satie was an excellent cook, so they decided there was no hurry to be on the road.

One night at dinner, Jode announced that he'd collected enough meat to last through esan, and he wouldn't need to do any more hunting. With a glance at her friends, Squint said that it was perfect timing, because she and her friends really did need to be on their way.

As a going away gesture, Satie made a special meal, including a freshly baked fruit pie for dessert. Both Satie and Jode said they would miss the three friends when they left. Jode, with a pointed looked at Cookie, who had spent the entire visit following Squint around, said, "All three of us."

The following morning, after a big breakfast, many hugs, and a promise to come back for a visit, Squint, Vayan and Beldon headed back to the road.

A few nights later, when it was time to camp, they noticed a small rise just off to the east, and they headed that way to look for a suitable place. As they came over the rise they could see flames farther to the east. Whatever it was, it was big. It was fairly close, so they decided to go see what was burning.

It didn't take them long to get to a scene of total devastation. There was wood and debris everywhere. There was a horse and some cows wandering around. A weeping woman was sitting on the ground, with two toddlers clinging to her. There was a man standing next to them, just staring at a fiercely burning building.

Beldon headed for the family, while Squint stopped dead where she was. She closed her eyes, created a shower big enough to cleanse the Giant of Beddon, and dumped it on the burning building.

There was a loud whoosh, and a massive cloud of smoke billowed up.

The fire was out, and it looked like she may have even been quick enough to save part of the house.

Indeed, two rooms of the house had survived with almost no damage. The family would be able to sleep under a roof tonight. They introduced themselves as the Stasla family. Mr. Stasla said that a man had come to the door and asked for some food. They had invited him in and fed him.

As he was getting ready to leave, he asked Mrs. Stasla if her daughter had any talents. Mrs. Stasla told him that females couldn't have talents, so of course she didn't. Although they weren't sure why, this must have angered the man. He turned to leave, but as he reached the top of the rise, he turned and casually flicked his hand. When he did, the house burst into flame.

After helping the family clean up their farm, they spent the night there, and set out again in the morning.

Beldon looked at Squint and said, "The Magician." It was what they were all thinking. With a shiver, Squint realized that he must be very close.

CHAPTER 19

With stops at two more homesteads, it took them nearly three weeks to get to Sella. It was late and snowing when they arrived.

They had talked earlier and decided it would be best if they stayed in Sella until dwowen. They would have far better luck finding shelter and work in a town, even a town this small, than they would taking their chances on the road.

They had no trouble finding an inn, and were glad to get out of the snow. At least at first. The gentleman behind the desk was a bit brusque.

"What?" he barked, as they came in the door.

Glancing at her friends, Squint said, "We're looking for rooms."

He glared at Squint and barked an outrageous price.

Squint, looking at her friends again, said, "Oh. Well, can we just get one room to share?"

With another glare at them, the man reached behind him and pulled a key from a board full of keys. He waited for Squint to pay him, slapped the key on the desk and snapped, "Up the stairs, last room on the right. And I don't want to hear any noise from you."

The room was small, and the bed was, too. Vayan took one look at the bed and said, "Squint, you can have the bed. You're the only one that'll fit on it."

Beldon looked around at the tiny room and said, "Can you believe what we're paying for this?"

"We're not going to be able to stay here again," said Squint. "We can't afford it. Tonight's room cost most of what we had left."

When they left the inn the next morning, they discovered that there wasn't much snow, and the clouds had all gone.

They had initially planned on asking the innkeeper if there was work available in town, but decided to look for a library or town hall and ask there. As they wandered the town, they found that the innkeeper wasn't the only one in town with an attitude. People they encountered would cross the street to avoid them. Some even turned around and went back the way they had come.

The town was small enough that it didn't take long to find the library. When they entered, there was a young lady just inside the door. She looked startled, turned to a young man behind the desk, and then turned around and left the library, very carefully not looking at Squint and her friends as she went by. Sharing a look, the three headed for the young man at the desk.

Although the young man wasn't quite as blatantly rude as the innkeeper, he came close.

"What is it you want," he said.

"We were hoping you could give us some information about the town," Squint said. "We're looking for work and a place to stay until dwowen."

The door opened, and a very large man wearing a uniform and badge entered.

"Need any help here, Coren?"

"I'm fine, Sheriff. I was just telling these people that we don't hire outsiders," the young man said.

"We're perfectly capable of taking care of our own," said the Sheriff. "You're best off heading for Belt. They'll be more likely to need help."

"Belt? Where's that?" asked Vayan.

"It's north of here, about two days' walk," said the librarian.

"Come with me," said the Sheriff. "I'll show you the way out of town."

When the Sheriff left them on the outskirts of town, they looked at each other, and Squint burst out laughing.

"What's so funny, Squint? Now we have two more days of walking before we can find a place to spend esan," grumbled Vayan.

"Yes, but didn't they make you feel like you have horns and a tail, or something? I mean, the town is right on the road. They must get travelers all the time. What is it about us that upset them so?"

Vayan grinned, and said, "You have a point. I guess it's all in the way you look at it."

"The sheriff marched us out of town like we were dangerous criminals," said Beldon. And then he chuckled. "I guess it is kind of funny."

The weather cooperated and stayed clear for the trip to Belt. When they arrived, it was mid-day, and the small town was bustling. They got a much different reception here than they had in Sella. People smiled and greeted them as they went by.

An older man stepped out of a building as they passed by. He was very large, with very red hair. He smiled, and said, "Hello. My name's Biren Wakes. Can I help you find something?"

"Hello, Mr. Wakes," said Squint. "People call me Squint, and these are my friends Vayan and Beldon." She smiled at the man and said, "We're doing some traveling and are hoping we can find work and a place to stay for a bit."

"Well, then it's lucky I needed a break," said Mr. Wakes. "I'm the mayor here. The town's small enough, I pretty much know who's doing what to whom." He laughed. "Everybody calls me Red, and you're welcome to do the same. What kind of work are you looking for?"

"Just about anything," said Squint. "We're not afraid of hard work."

"Well, when you're not traveling, what do you do?" he asked.

"Well, Vayan here is a superb furniture maker, and Beldon is the best li-, uh, teacher you ever met. I just finished school, so I don't do anything in particular yet. But we're all good at following directions."

"I'm sure we can find something for you." Red smiled, and said, "Come on in, out of the cold. We'll have some lunch and talk about what's available."

As in Ander, Squint seemed to have lucked out and found just the right person to help them as soon they arrived in town.

Once inside, Red grinned at their reaction. They had entered a huge room. The room had all the equipment for furniture making, with a number of pieces of partially finished furniture scattered around.

"It's a small town, and being mayor doesn't take much time, so I'm also the local furniture maker," he said. "I'm hoping you meant what you said about Vayan being an excellent furniture maker, because I could sure use a hand."

They wove their way through the room to a small door in the back. He opened the door and stepped back for them to enter.

"I live back here," he said. "I have a pot of stew on the stove, and some freshly baked bread. We can eat while we talk about what's best for you."

Once they were all seated at the kitchen table with bowls of stew and slices of bread, Red looked at Vayan and said, "So are you really a furniture maker?"

"Yes, Sir," Vayan replied. I love making beautiful furniture, and I'm very good at it."

"Would you be willing to help me out here?" asked Red. "I can pay you a fair wage."

"I would like that a lot, Sir," said Vayan, with a big smile.

Red frowned at Vayan, and said, "There is one condition."

"What's that, Sir?" asked Vayan.

"Stop calling me Sir!"

"Yes, Si—uh, Red." Everyone laughed.

"Good, that's taken care of. Now let's see what we can do for you two," said Red. "Squint said you're a teacher, is that right, Beldon?"

"Well, I was a teacher," Beldon responded. "But to tell the truth, I didn't like it much." He glanced at Squint and said, "A good friend recently suggested that I'd make a much better librarian than teacher, and I'm inclined to think he might be right. I've spent a great many hours in libraries, including working as a librarian's assistant, and I love everything about them."

"Well, that's okay, because we don't need a teacher. The one we have is excellent. Let me talk to Jin. He's our librarian, and can probably put you to good use," said Red. "I'll have to check to see how much we can pay, though."

"Now Squint," said Red. "You said you just got out of school, and don't do anything. What have you been doing while you've been traveling?"

"Well, I have a small healing talent, but I won't charge for that. I've been doing small chores like cooking, cleaning and household repairs," Squint responded.

"You do healing without charging?" asked Red. "Why? If you're any good, you could make some really good money."

"I wouldn't feel right doing that," Squint frowned and said, "If someone is in need of healing, they shouldn't be thinking about money. I can make my money in other ways."

Red thought for a moment, and then said, "I'll tell you what I'll do for you, Squint. I'll put the word out that you're available for healings. I know of a number of people that need a good healer, but can't afford it. Assuming you're any good, I'm sure we can keep you busy. The town will pay you a small fee for each healing. That way, the town gets healthy, and you get paid." He looked at her, and said, "Will that work for you?"

"I don't want you to take this the wrong way, but why would you do all this for people you don't know?" Squint asked.

"Oh, I'm not doing it for you," Red said. "I love my town, and I will do anything to make the people's lives easier. If I can help out others while I'm providing for the town, then so much the better." He grinned and said, "Besides, I like you."

"Beats the reception we got in Sella," said Vayan sourly.

"You stopped in Sella? No one stops there unless they have to," said Red. "There's something wrong in that town. It's like something's gotten hold of the people there and turned them all mean."

They finished their meal, and Vayan offered to wash the dishes. Beldon laughed, and said, "If you like your dishes, don't let him wash them. You be lucky if they survive. Let me."

Everyone chatted while Beldon cleared the table and washed the dishes. When he finished, Red said, "Come sit, Beldon. We still have one more thing to discuss."

Beldon returned to the table, and the three looked questioningly at Red.

"The only thing left is to find you a place to stay," said Red. "It should be a place with plenty of room for you to stay together, and where Squint can do his healing. One that isn't going to cost you a fortune."

"Here's my suggestion," he said. "And this is just a suggestion. You don't have to do this." He looked a bit uncomfortable for a moment, and then said, "My mother lives alone in the old house I grew up in." He looked down at the table, and continued. "She's getting on a bit, and can't do as much as she used to, although she doesn't like to admit it. It's a pretty big house, and needs some work."

He looked up at them, and said, "I know this is a lot to ask of you, but if you could stay at the house while you're here, and maybe do some chores for her, I would be very grateful."

He looked around, and said, "I wouldn't charge you anything to stay there."

Squint looked at Vayan and Beldon, who both nodded back at her. She turned to Red and said, "Okay, but now *we* have a condition."

Looking a bit worried, he asked, "What condition?".

"You must charge us a fair rent."

The home that Red took them to was in the center of town. It was big, the biggest home they'd seen so far. It was two stories and had a large yard, but everything was a bit run down.

They entered into a small foyer. On their right, they could see an open dining area. In front of them was a hallway. On the left was a closed door. Red explained that this was his mother's bedroom. He told them that it had once been a playroom, but had been converted to a bedroom, so that his mother didn't need to go upstairs every day.

Red led them forward through the hall, which held the stairs to the upper level. Past the hall, they entered a sitting area. To the left of this was a small library, and on their right was the kitchen. This is where they found Red's mother.

She was tiny. Even smaller than Squint when she wasn't disguised as a boy. Her hair was mostly white, but still had streaks of faded red, making it apparent where Red had gotten his red hair.

Red leaned down—way down--and gave her a hug. Looking at the two of them together, it was hard to believe that this tiny woman could have given birth to the huge man next to her. But it was clear that the two cared a great deal for each other.

"Mom, I need to ask you a favor," said Red.

"Of course, Dear. What can I do for you?"

"These young people need a place to stay for a while. Do you think you could put them up here?" asked Red.

"Well, let me think. It's pretty crowded here, and there isn't much space," she said, with a serious look on her face. "But I guess we could all make do."

She grinned and said, "Biren, of course they can stay here. It will be lovely to have young people in the house again."

"Thank you, Mrs. Wakes. We'll do our best to stay out of your way," Vayan said.

"Oh, do call me Leela. Mrs. Wakes sounds so stuffy,' she said. "And I'd much rather you don't stay out of my way. I wasn't just being polite when I said it would be nice to have young people in the house again."

So the three moved into the Wakes home.

Vayan spent his days in Red's workshop, building and repairing furniture.

Beldon spent mornings at the library with Jin, who was excited to have someone with whom he could share his duties and his love of the library. The two spent as much time chatting and becoming friends as they did taking care of the library.

He spent the rest of his time doing odd jobs for Leela and a number of her elderly friends around town, mostly free of charge.

Squint was kept busy providing healing. She usually went to the customer, rather than having them come to her. And, since many of her customers were elderly, she spent quite a bit of time doing household chores and minor repairs, as well as healing. She charged the city the agreed-upon price for the healing, but never charged for the "extras" she provided.

She did find time to visit the library to continue her research into the final confrontation. Like the library in Anders, there were several books on the subject which were interesting to read, but none that contained any useful information.

They also continued to find time to visit the magic training room at the Kenna Academy to work on their talents, as they had been since the boys had joined her on her travels.

Red had dinner with them most nights, and the three friends came to feel like the Wakes were almost family.

They learned that Red had two elder siblings. His oldest brother was a musician, and had moved to Melsta to better his chances at making a living with his music. Over the years, he had done quite well, and achieved a modicum of fame.

When Red's older sister had linked, she moved to Norla with her new husband. They had three children, and were quite happy. The family came to visit once or twice a year.

Squint was home alone with Leela one afternoon. She was sitting beside her on a couch surreptitiously giving her a light healing. She said, "Leela, I don't mean to be nosy, but what happened to your husband?"

"Oh, my dear, you could never be nosy. You're far too sweet to do anything offensive." She patted Squint's hand, which was resting on her shoulder, and said, "I still get sad when I think about it."

"My Ail was a wonderful husband. He was so handsome. Actually, Biren looks a lot like him," she said with a sigh. "Ail was a fisherman and owned his own boat. When Fraisir, our youngest son, finished school, he joined Ail on his boat. Being a fisherman like his father was all Fraisir ever wanted to do."

"About fifteen years ago," she continued, "they were out at sea when a huge storm came up unexpectedly. Ail and Fraisir never returned, and no one ever found any sign of them or the boat."

Adding a bit of comfort to her healing, Squint leaned over and gave Leela a big hug. "That had to have been terrible," she said. "Not knowing, I mean."

"That was the hardest," said Leela. "I kept waiting and hoping for years." She looked at Squint and said, "If I tell you something, will you keep it to yourself?"

"Of course," said Squint.

"I worry that Biren only stays here in Belt because of me. I want nothing more than for him to be truly happy, and I sometimes think that he would be happier if he went to a bigger city, like his brother and sister did. Maybe he could find a wife and start a family of his own." She sighed, and said, "Maybe I'm just being an old woman, and worrying for nothing."

"Well," said Squint, "if you want my opinion, I think he's very happy here. I know he loves his furniture business, and being mayor of Belt. I don't think he would be happy anywhere else."

Leela looked closely at Squint and said, "You really mean that, don't you?" With tears in her eyes, she hugged Squint and said, "You know, I'm really going to hate it when you leave here."

Over dinner one night in early dwowen, Red asked the friends if they enjoyed watching squares. All three responded with enthusiasm.

"That was one of our favorite activities at the academy," said Vayan. "We spend many happy hours watching together."

"Do any of you play?" Red asked.

"I'm too small," said Squint, "Beldon is much happier watching than playing, and Vayan thinks his talent constitutes cheating, so he won't play."

"Well, I'm kind of an unofficial assistant coach for the school, and since squares has started for the season, I thought you might enjoy watching some of the games" said Red. "We also have enough men in town that we form up several teams each dwowen, and hold our own competition."

"That sounds like fun," said Squint, while Vayan and Beldon both nodded in agreement.

Red looked at Vayan and said, "You should join us for the competition, Vayan. On my team, of course. I'm sure you've learned to control your talent enough to play without using it, and I'd like to be on the winning team this year."

"Oh, I don't know," said Vayan, with a frown. He glanced at Squint and said, "It actually sounds great, but I'm not sure how much longer we're going to be here."

"Would it be okay if he played until we're ready to move on?" asked Squint.

"I'm sure we can work that out, if you're really interested in playing," said Red. "I would really love having you on my team."

Red arranged everything with the other teams, and Vayan was happy to join Red's team. After that, the three friends spent several evenings a week watching either the school squares team, or the adult's competition.

Midden was almost over when Squint finally decided that she had procrastinated long enough. It was well past time for her to move on. She sensed that she had learned all that she could here in Belt, and she was also sure that she was as prepared as she would ever be for the final confrontation.

In addition to the daily activities of which her friends were aware, Squint had been doing some traveling. She had been visiting libraries and museums across the country, researching everything she could about the Magician, the Receptacle, and the final confrontation.

All of her research had led to her acknowledgement of something that she had always known, but had been unwilling to admit. The final confrontation would be between her and the Magician. Alone. No matter how much she wanted it to be different, she was not going to be able to rely on her friends for help. And she didn't know how to tell them.

That afternoon, Squint sat down on the porch swing next to Vayan, as the three friends relaxed before dinner. Squint glanced nervously at her friends, and said, "Hey, guys?"

"I don't like that look." said Vayan. "Why do I get the impression you're going to say something we don't like?"

"Well, I guess I am," Squint said. "It's time for me to get moving." She paused for a moment, looked down at her lap, and said, "I can't stay here forever."

Vayan sighed deeply and said, "Yeah, I guess I knew this was coming."

Squint took Vayan's hand, and said, "I think that Beldon and I both know how you feel about Red, Vayan."

"Although I haven't talked to Beldon about this, I think that he'll agree with what I'm thinking." She looked at Beldon, and then back at Vayan. "I think you should stay here."

She shifted so she was directly facing Vayan and said, "Look Vayan, this is exactly what you were looking for when we left Kenna. You and Red get along famously, and you love what you're doing here. And," she grinned at him, "your squares team is in the lead. You will never find a place that suits you so well."

Beldon shifted forward on his chair and said, "Vayan, you know Squint's right. This is where you belong."

"I know, I know," said Vayan, "but what about the Magician? I can't just abandon Squint."

"Vayan, if you stay here, you won't be abandoning me," said Squint. "Look, when the time comes, I am quite capable of coming and collecting you."

She shifted back on the swing, looked at each of her friends, and said, "Here's the thing. We have no idea when or where we'll meet the Magician. It could be years before we find him. In the meantime, we need to get on with our lives."

She looked at Beldon, and then back at Vayan. "You both know I'm right. Right now, I think you, Vayan, are exactly where you should be."

She turned and grinned at Beldon and said, "I'm hoping there will come a time when Beldon finds a place that suits him just as well."

"Once I find the Magician, I am quite capable of finding both of you and bringing you to my side." Knowing she would be doing nothing of the sort made saying that feel dishonest. Although the way she worded it wasn't *exactly* a lie, it still *felt* like a lie. It hurt her to the core to be telling her two best friends such an untruth, but she could not bring herself to tell them that she believed that, if she should bring them to the final confrontation, they would be sacrificing themselves for nothing.

At that moment, Leela came out to announce that dinner was ready.

As everyone was finishing their dinner, Squint said, "Before everyone leaves, I'd like to make an announcement."

"As much as we love it here, it is time for us to be moving on."

She reached across the table and touched Leela's hand. "You are such a special person, Leela, and we will miss you enormously.

Red, you are like a father to us all, and I can't express how much this time with you has meant to us."

Red looked down at the table and said, rather sheepishly, "I must say, I've begun to think of Vayan almost as my son. I was selfishly hoping he would stay here and join my business."

Vayan reached across the table and squeezed Red's big hands. "Honestly, I'd like nothing better," he said. He glanced at his friends and said, "The three of us talked about this, and we all agreed that, if you were all right with it, I'd like to stay." With a big grin, he said, "It seems that you're all right with it."

CHAPTER 20

After much discussion, Beldon and Squint had decided that their goal now was to find the Magician, and that they were most likely to find him in one of the bigger cities. With that in mind, they would take the most direct route to Norla, with as few stops as possible.

One night, while they ate dinner by firelight, Beldon commented that they might get lucky and get a chance to observe the Magician without his knowledge. They might be able to learn something that would give them an edge in the upcoming battle

Squint thought about this a lot over the next few days. She believed the Magician must be getting impatient for the encounter with the Receptacle. At this point, he had to know the Receptacle was aware of him, and would most likely be openly searching for her.

She did not believe it would be possible to catch the Magician off guard. And even if they did, the likelihood of learning something useful was extremely unlikely.

A week or so later, they were nearing Norla. They had passed through Greyn, but had only stayed for a few days. They wanted to move on to Norla as soon as possible. If they didn't find the Magician in Norla, they would travel to Melsta. If they didn't find him in Melsta, they could continue west from there.

Before they arrived in Norla, they had decided that they would look for daily work doing odd jobs, rather than committing to long-term obligations, as they had in Belt. This would give them more opportunities to pick up information about the Magician.

Once they arrived in Norla, however, they realized that this might not be all that easy. Norla was nearly as large as Melsta, and spread out over a huge area. Like Melsta, it was sure to have many libraries. Finding the best place to get information about available work for them might be difficult.

They arrived mid-day and decided to look around until they found suitable lodgings for their stay. In addition to giving them an area of town in which to center their search for work, the cost of their lodgings would tell them how much money they would need to make at any job they took. At Beldon's insistence, however, the first thing they looked for was a place to eat.

Squint had decided to drop her disguise and just be herself. Although it was probably best to keep the disguise while traveling, it should be safe to drop it while in town. Consequently, she was wearing a dress and her braid hung loosely down her back. Beldon found it difficult to address this attractive young lady as Squint, but he supposed he would get used to it.

They stopped at the first restaurant they came upon. It was a small place, but appeared to be busy. Hopefully, that meant they served good food.

Within in minutes of arriving, they were seated at a table by a window, and Squint was chatting with the waitress like they were best friends. Beldon had always been a bit shy, and it amazed him how easily Squint chatted with perfect strangers.

While Squint and the waitress chatted, he looked around the restaurant. Although he was happy that Vayan had found such a suitable place with Red, he missed him. Working at the library in Belt had proven to him that working in a library was what he wanted to do with his life, and he was looking forward to a time when he could look for a permanent place to settle. He could only hope that he could find something as perfect for him as Vayan had found for himself.

After a few minutes, he realized that a number of men were focusing on his table. He turned to see what they were staring at. He studied the waitress and decided that, although she was pleasant to look at, she didn't warrant the kind of attention their table was receiving.

He looked around at the other tables again and realized that the men were looking at Squint, not the waitress.

He turned back to look at Squint. She was listening intently to whatever the waitress was saying to her. Her hair hung down her back in a tidy braid, the reddish-brown color lightened by her time in the sun. There was nothing remarkable about the dress she wore, but it fit her snuggly, and accented her figure. Which, he realized, was very attractive.

He looked back at Squint, and thought, "Squint is not only pretty, he's beautiful." This thought made him grin.

But it also made him realize that it really was a good idea for Squint to appear as a boy while they traveled. Looking like that, he--no, she--was bound to draw unwanted attention. He wondered if she knew how beautiful she was.

"Hey, Beldon, are you listening?" asked Squint.

Squint and the waitress were looking at him strangely. It made him realize that he was staring at Squint.

"Beldon, said Squint, "are you okay?"

Now Squint was looking at him with concern. "I'm sorry, I'm fine", he said. "What did you need?"

Still looking at him strangely, Squint said, "Vaita was telling me that she knows of a good boarding house where we can stay. It's very nice, inexpensive, and the proprietor will provide an excellent breakfast and dinner for a bit extra."

"Sounds perfect," he said.

"How does he--she do it," he thought. "We get to a town, and the first person she talks to has just the information we need. Maybe it's another talent," he thought, grinning again.

Squint and Beldon enjoyed a leisurely lunch, and then followed Vaita's excellent directions to the boarding house she had suggested.

The boarding house was a large, one-story building. The yard was large and well cared for. There was a huge front porch with a comfortable-looking porch swing, and several chairs scattered around.

Vaita was right. The accommodations were pleasant, and the proprietor was delightful. He was a large young man, with curly black hair and a full beard and mustache. He introduced himself as Alfer Jens, and he immediately made them feel welcome.

He said they had timed it just right, because two rooms had just become available. The rooms he showed them were small, but immaculate. They were beautifully decorated, and had everything needed for a comfortable stay.

He invited them to the kitchen, where they could have tea while they discussed details.

The prices were reasonable. As long as it didn't take too long, they would have enough money to last until they found work.

Squint and Beldon stayed in Norla until dwowen. They had no trouble finding work. They kept busy, and made enough to allow them to live quite comfortably.

The two of them spent most of their time doing odd jobs. Squint also provided healing when she could and Beldon spent his extra time helping out in the nearest library. They visited Vaita at the restaurant often, and spent many pleasant evenings sitting on the front porch of the boarding house with Alfer.

When it was time to leave, they decided they would travel to Melsta. They needed to find the Magician, and Melsta was the most sensible place to go. Although he might not actually be in Melsta, thinking about his behavior at the farm south of Sella, there were likely to be more such incidents, and Melsta was the most likely place to hear about them.

Rather than traveling straight to Melsta, they decided to visit Vayan. After, saying their goodbyes, Squint took them to Belt. It was mid-afternoon when they got to the furniture shop, but there was no one there. After a bit of discussion, they decided there must be a game of squares going on, and headed for the field.

Sure enough, they arrived in the middle of a game. The stands were packed, and the only empty seats were at the top of the stadium. They make their way up, and settled in to watch the game.

As was usual for her, Squint spent as much time watching the people in the stands as she did watching the game. She eventually noticed a very attractive young lady across the stadium from her who seemed to be focused on Vayan. She would jump up and cheer whenever he made a play, even if the play was insignificant.

Once the game finished, she hopped her way down the stands and on to the playing field, rushing to Vayan and giving him a big hug.

When Squint and Beldon were finally able to reach Vayan, they found him holding the young lady firmly to his side. Vayan introduced her as Joyen Herm. She was tall, her head reaching almost to Vayan's shoulder. She had long, red hair, and bright, blue eyes. She was very pretty.

When Vayan introduced Squint and Beldon, her face brightened and she said, "Oh, I've -been looking forward to meeting you. Vayan talks about you all the time.

After Joyen left later that afternoon, the three were enjoying a drink on the porch at the Wakes house. Squint said that Joyen seemed to be very nice. Vayan grinned and said, "I hoped you would like her, because I think she's nice enough that I'd like to ask her to be my wife."

He said Joyen lived with her mother, and helped out with her younger siblings. The youngest was nearly finished with school, so she wouldn't be needed for much longer. She hadn't settled on what she would do when that time came.

He said he'd found a vacant lot that was near the furniture shop and Belt's school. It was large, and had trees that provided a sense of privacy. It was inexpensive, and he wanted to build a house there to present to Joyen after their linking. The problem is, he didn't want to desert Leela Wakes.

"Have you talked to Joyen about it?" Squint asked. "I know you want to surprise her, but don't you think your future wife would like a say in where you'll be living?"

Vayan continued to think about Squint's comment long after his friends left. When he finally asked Joyen to be his wife, he also discussed his idea for a house with her. Her reaction left him no doubt that Squint had been right about asking Joyen before making a decision.

Joyen's family all lived in Belt, but they wanted to be able to invite all of Vayan's family to the linking. His family would need a place to stay while they were there, and it would be nice if they could stay at the Wakes house.

They met with Red and Leela one night to give them the news, and to ask them about Vayan's family.

The first thing they did was invite Red and Leela to the linking. Once Leela was done crying, they asked her about having Vayan's family stay at the house. She was so happy that they thought her house good enough to invite family, that she started crying again. Joyen gave Leela her pocket towel, since Leela's was soaked.

Once Leela had finish crying again, and had tried to return Joyen's pocket towel (which Joyen didn't want back), Vayan brought up the subject of where they would live once they were linked. He was a bit worried about hurting Leela's feelings now.

Leela looked at him and asked, "Would you live in this house, if you could?"

Glancing at Joyen, Vayan said, "Leela, we love you, both of us. But we don't want to start our life together living with someone else."

"Oh, you silly boy. I wouldn't want you to. No, that would just not do. What I'm suggesting is that, if you want it, I would like to give the house to you. As a gift."

At the astonished looks on their faces, Leela continued. "Vayan, you are like a grandson to me. Like Red's son. And I would be honored to have you live here and raise a family. Red has been begging me to move in with him for years. And since it doesn't look like he's going to find a wife any time soon, I would like to take him up on his offer."

Now it was Joyen who was crying, and Vayan was working hard to keep his tears at bay. When Vayan looked at Joyen, she nodded. Vayan got up from his chair and went to Leela. He gently lifted from her chair, and hugged her.

"You have no idea how happy you've made us. We would like nothing better than to raise a family in this house."

CHAPTER 21

Squint was pretty sure she could take them to a spot just outside the Gendry Hedge Maze. It was very unlikely that anything about the maze would have changed, so if they traveled early in the morning, there should be no problem.

There should have been no problem, but she must have miscalculated slightly. They ended up IN the hedges of the maze, rather than near them. She immediately took them back where they started, and then tried again.

This time was better, but still not perfect. They weren't inside the hedges, but they were inside the maze.

Beldon had several scratches on the back of his hands, and one fairly large one on his cheek. Squint had some leaves and twigs in her hair, but was unharmed.

"I'm sorry Beldon. I'm not sure how I got that wrong," she said.

"Well, it has been a long time since you've been here." Beldon smiled at her. "There was no real harm, so I forgive you." He grinned down at her.

By the time they worked their way out of the maze, it was late enough that they should be able to find something to eat at the outdoor markets. They took their time, and enjoyed wandering around, looking at the great assortment of things for sale, and watching the variety of people shopping.

They finally selected something from the many choices of food, and headed to the Gendry Fountain to eat. Even though it was near the end of midden, the weather was mild. They sat for much longer than they intended to, just enjoying doing nothing.

Beldon still found himself surprised when men took an interest in Squint. While they traveled, and when they visited Vayan, Squint was always in her male disguise. And she didn't always remember to drop the disguise when they got to a town. He spent far more time with Squint than he did with Serran, so he tended to forget how beautiful Serran was.

Beldon suspected that, had he not been sitting next to her, a number of the men that had passed by would have stopped to talk to Squint.

Finally, they agreed it was time to search for a place to stay. This time, Squint's ability to find just the right person to help them seemed to have failed. It took them almost a week, and a couple of really nasty places, to find a suitable place to stay.

They wanted to spend esan in Melsta. When it got close to dwowen, they could decide what to do next.

They were doing odd jobs, but since they were planning on staying a while, they wanted to look for more substantial work.

Beldon started visiting libraries, hoping to find a position. Squint wasn't sure what she should look for, so she decided to continue taking odd jobs until she found something suitable.

The two would meet at the boarding house at the end of each day. The boarding house didn't provide meals, so they would change clothes and then go find something to eat. They chose a different restaurant each evening. They felt this would be a good way to become familiar with Melsta, which would hopefully help them find positions. Besides, it was fun.

It was around three weeks after they arrived that Beldon came home visibly excited.

"Let's get dressed up for dinner tonight," He said. "I've got some good news to share."

Squint, having seen how excited Beldon was, decided to take great care in dressing up. Some time ago, she had found the most beautiful gown she had ever seen. It was a deep green color, with pale green lace at the waist, neckline and wrists. It was full length, with a broad, sweeping skirt.

She had spent more on this dress than she had ever spent on a piece of clothing before. In fact, she had spent more on it than she usually spent on clothing in a year. When she bought it, she had popped back to her grandmother's house and stored it in a chest.

She pulled her birthday stone out of its usual nesting place against her chest, added some fancy shoes and, for the final touch, unbraided her hair and let it flow down her back.

When she met Beldon downstairs, he was stunned by how beautiful she was.

"Some day, some man is going to be awfully lucky," he thought.

He, too, had gotten dressed up. He was wearing a beautifully cut grey suit and dress shoes. He had made an attempt to tame his dark curls, and it looked like he had even taken the time to trim his beard.

"Now we just need somewhere fancy to eat," he said.

As he said this, Srenya, the owner of the boarding house, came around the corner. He whistled at them, and said, "Where are you two going, all dressed up?"

"We don't know," said Beldon. "We're looking for a special place to spend a special occasion. Do you know of anywhere suitable?"

"Well, it depends on how much you're willing to spend," he said. "I know of a place that would be perfect, but it's very expensive."

"That sounds like just what we're looking for," said Beldon.

When they arrived at the restaurant Srenya had recommended, Squint whispered to Beldon, "Are you sure you can afford this place, Beldon?"

"I'm sure," he grinned.

The restaurant was elegant, with crystal chandeliers, white linens, and silver tableware.

The waiters were all dressed in suits, and the patrons were even more elaborately dressed than Beldon and Squint were.

Their waiter arrived and handed them a menu. He gave them a few moments to look at their menus, and then, with a heavy Tayran accent, said "Might I suggest the chef's special, which is . . ."

Beldon and Squint shared a glance, and then both nodded to the waiter. "That will be fine," said Beldon.

When he left, Squint, stifling laughter, looked at Beldon. Beldon actually had his hand pressed to his mouth to prevent his laughter.

"I have no idea what we just ordered," he giggled.

"I think it might be fish," Squint said, "but I'm not sure. I'm afraid I couldn't understand what he said."

"I have no idea what half the things on the menu are," said Beldon.

"Well, I understood the words, but I did not know that some of those things were edible." That was enough to make Squint laugh out loud, just loud enough to attract attention from the nearby tables.

She put a hand over her mouth to stifle more laughter. Beldon noticed that this time, Squint's, or rather Serran's, beauty and smiling animation had attracted the attention of as many women as men. She really was quite beautiful.

When the waiter returned with their dinner, which was indeed a beautifully cooked gotfish, he was very attentive to Squint, inquiring if the food was to her liking, if the wine was acceptable, and if there was anything else he could get her.

He finally turned to Beldon, asked briefly if everything was to his satisfaction, glanced again at Squint, and reluctantly left the table.

Still smiling hugely, Squint said, "Okay, now what's the big news?"

"Do you remember the library with the wonderful lightroofs that we visited with the academy?" he asked.

Squint nodded, and he went on, "I went there today. I didn't go to look for work, but to see if they found someone to filter the lightroofs. I found out that they did find someone. She is willing to apply the filter to the lightroofs, but she isn't a librarian, and has no desire to work in a library," he said.

"That's great," said Squint, "It would be terrible to have to cover up those beautiful lightroofs. But I assume that's not what has you so excited."

"No, you're right. You're not going to believe what happened," he exclaimed. His earlier excitement returning, Beldon continued. "I met Master Peyta while I was there. He actually remembered me!"

Between their waiter's many over-attentive interruptions, Beldon finally got to the point.

"Beginning tomorrow, I will be the new Head Librarian at the Melsta Library of Light."

Squint let out a short squeal, and reached for Beldon's hands. "That is absolutely the most wonderful news," she said. "No wonder you're so excited."

It turns out that the head librarian that was hired shortly after the Kenna students' visit had left, and Master Peyta had been assisting at the library while they searched for a new one. It turned out that Master Peyta not only remembered Beldon, but he remembered thinking it was a waste that Beldon was to be a teacher, with his love for libraries.

He would start tomorrow, and Master Peyta would continue to assist for a time, while Beldon got adjusted to his new position.

It only took a few weeks for Squint to realize that Beldon had found the perfect position. It took much longer for Beldon to realize it.

At dinner one evening, he said to Squint, "You know, when I was at the academy, I would never have dreamed I could be this happy."

He dipped his head, and thought for a moment. "I was never close to my family, and they never visited me while I was at the academy, so I don't really miss them. I miss Vayan, but you see to it that I see him regularly, so I don't miss him too much."

Glancing at Squint, he continued, "I've made some wonderful new friends, and I don't think I could ever find a job more suited to me."

Looking back down at the table, he said, "I guess what I'm saying is that I'd like to stay here is Melsta until it's time to fight the Magician."

Reaching across the table to take Beldon's hands, Squint said, "I wondered how long it would take you to figure that out."

At the look on his face, Squint laughed out loud.

"You mean you don't mind?"

"Beldon, while we were in Belt, I said that I was hoping you would find something that suited you as well as Vayan was suited to the position he found with Red. I meant what I said. There is no point in all of us wasting our lives trying to find the Magician. I am sure he will find me when the time is right."

Once again lying to her friend, and hating it, she added, "When he does, I will come get you and Vayan. In the meantime, we should all get on with our lives."

CHAPTER 22

Squint visited Vayan and Beldon every week or so. With Beldon working at the library in Melsta, she was able to check out a few books each visit. Mostly, she selected text books, but she always included one or two books from the fiction section.

Last night, she read a book about a young girl who found a baby kell and followed it to its tribe. She ended up lost, and remained with the kell for many years, learning to communicate with them.

An amusing story, but Squint had met kell close up. There was nothing about a kell, baby or adult, that would prompt a young girl to want to follow it.

They were ugly beasts, and they smelled. They had tiny eyes, huge ears, and a long, skinny snout. Their hair was long, dirty and tangled. And they were massive. When down on four feet, an adult was taller than Squint. Standing on two feet, they were one of the most frightening beasts Squint had ever seen.

As far as Squint could tell, the only sound they made was a deep, gravelly growl. And it was loud. Very loud. This sound appeared to be made only when the kell wanted to threaten. And they apparently liked to threaten--anything that came near them. These were not cuddly, friendly beasts.

Squint had seen several tribes on her travels in the northwest. She spent nearly a week in the vicinity of the kell, and had heard that nasty growl almost constantly.

To amuse herself while she walked today, she had been trying to recreate that sound, without much success. She would get close, but then it would break up. It sounded like her kell was a bit sick. Just for amusement, she tried making the sound come from different places. She got pretty good at making it sound close or far away, and making it sound like it was coming from various directions.

As she looked around, she realized that it was getting dark, and looked like it might rain. She moved farther off the road, into the woods, to find a place to sleep for the night. It didn't take long to find what looked like the perfect spot.

Two large trees had fallen in such a way that they left a nice hollow spot between them. Using her traveling cloak, she covered an area big enough she should stay dry. As she arranged the cloak, it reminded her of her first attempt at making a traveling cloak.

When she, Vayan and Beldon had first begun to talk about traveling together to find the magician, she had decided to make them matching traveling cloaks. Since she wanted the cloaks to be a surprise for the boys, she had guessed at the measurements.

What were supposed to be magnificent, sweeping, royal blue cloaks, turned out to be rather narrow, dull grey cloaks. Beldon's cloak was too narrow in the shoulders and Vayan's cloak was too short. And even though she had measured hers, it somehow ended up far too long.

In addition, none of them was completely waterproof. Vayan's had a huge spot on the left shoulder that leaked, hers had a spot on the chest that leaked, and poor Beldon's leaked in a rather unfortunate area of the backside.

It took her several more tries, and a good deal of help from her grandmother, to finally get them right.

The one she had now, in addition to being practical and beautiful, was made with a sort of pocket on that upper back that accommodated the pack she carried. If she wasn't wearing her pack, it folded neatly, looking something like a small cape on the back of the coat.

She had settled in and was reading a large medical text when she sensed two men coming toward her. Although she could sense them, she couldn't see or hear them through the rain. She continued reading, but kept her senses alert.

Apparently, even though she wasn't able to see them, they could see her. They had stopped somewhere nearby, and were having a quiet discussion. This seemed a bit unusual, so she decided to "listen" to them, to see what they were up to.

"Look, whoever, it is, they don't look very big. I think we can take 'em. They're lookin' all comfortable, and I bet they have food."

"Okay, maybe we'll get lucky and they'll have some money, too. Just walk quiet, okay? Last time your big feet scared 'em away."

Squint *was* "all comfortable," so she decided to try using her kell growl. Maybe she could scare them away without having to get wet.

She started out with a few quiet growls. As soon as the two men heard the first growl, they stopped where they were.

"What was that?"

"Don't know. Sounded like that person made it."

"Don't be stupid. Let's go."

She tried another growl, a bit louder this time. And tried making it sound like it came from behind the men.

The location of the growl was right, but the growl itself sounded terrible. It came out all cracked and gravely. Since the idea was to frighten the men into leaving, that was okay with Squint.

Again, the two men stopped. By now, they were close enough that Squint could see a vague outline of them. She watched as they turned to look behind them.

"There it is again, but now it's over there."

"Is there more than one of them?"

"Let's just get this over with and get out of here."

Squint growled again, much louder, and changed the direction of the growl. This time, she made it sound like it was off to the west. And then again, louder yet, and without changing the direction, so it came from her.

"That's it. I'm getting out of here!"

"Me, too!"

No longer being quiet, the two men ran like the King of Doezin was after them. Squint let out a few more growls, just for fun, and then settled back in to finish reading her book.

CHAPTER 23

This was the longest Squint had stayed in one place since leaving Kenna. She had been here for almost two years. She knew she should move on and continue looking for the Magician, but she was tired. She needed time to relax and regroup. When she arrived here in the south-western town of Echan, she decided she would stay a while.

It was another one of many mid-sized towns she'd stayed in. It would be able to provide her with plenty of opportunities for work. Finding housing should be easy. And it was big enough to provide opportunities to work on her talents.

She found a house on her second day in town. Once again, she would be staying with an elderly woman who would provide cheap room and board to someone who would help around the house. Miss Selta Aagne was one of the sweetest people Squint had ever met, and she thought Squint was "just as cute as a curby".

It didn't take her long to establish herself as a healer. Once again, she did not charge for her healing services, so she also did odd jobs to make money.

Right now, Squint was tired, but rather pleased with herself. She had been here since first light, and it was now far past lunch time.

The young lady had sent her housewoman to Squint yesterday evening with a request for an appointment. The housewoman had explained that Miss Dens was very ill, and would like to see Miss Nylls as soon as possible. Although Squint usually spent the first hour of her day helping Miss Aagne, this sounded urgent, so she told the housewoman that she would be there first thing in the morning.

When Squint arrived at the house, the housewoman explained that Miss Dens was not yet ready for Squint. She asked if Squint would wait in the day room until Miss Dens was ready.

"What will you be doing while we wait," Squint asked.

The housewoman looked oddly at Squint and said, "I'll be working in the kitchen."

"Would it be all right of I joined you there? I'd much rather have company while I wait."

Although she didn't look happy about it, the housewoman agreed.

Once in the kitchen, the housewoman offered Squint a seat at the table.

"Oh, no,' said Squint. "I meant I would like to help with whatever you're doing. I'm not good at just sitting around."

"Well, I suppose that would be all right," said the housewoman. "My name's Jenda. We can start by getting these dishes clean, if that's all right with you."

"My name is Serran, and I'll be glad to help with whatever you need," Squint replied.

Over an hour later, the kitchen was clean, breakfast had been prepared, and they had gotten things underway for dinner tonight.

Squint had found out that the woman's name was Mrs. Jenda Landey, and that she had worked for the Dens family since she had been widowed, over twenty years ago. She had initially been hired by Lialey Dens' parents as a cleaning girl, and had worked her way up to housewoman. She had also told Squint that Lialey Dens was a difficult person, and that she would have quit long ago, had she not promised Lialey's parents that she would stay as long as Lialey needed her.

But, since none of this was what Squint had come here for, she finally told Jenda that she had other clients, and that Miss Dens would see her now, or she would have to make another appointment.

Having finally been escorted to Lialey Dens' bedroom, she was introduced to a sour-faced young woman lying in the middle of a huge bed, surrounded by a massive pile of lacy pillows.

The young lady said, "My name is Miss Dens." She then turned to Jenda and said, "Well don't just stand there, get us some tea."

Jenda quickly excused herself and left.

When Squint started to speak, Miss Dens interrupted her and said, "Why don't we wait until the housewoman returns, so we're not disturbed."

Once Jenda returned with the tea, she asked Miss Dens if she would like to get dressed. Miss Dens snapped back, "Can't you see that I'm having one of my bad days? You should know that I won't be good for anything today."

It took another frustrating half hour of adjusting pillows and replacing bedding before Miss Dens was satisfied that everything was ready to begin.

Squint suggested that Jenda didn't need to be there, and could go about her morning business, but Miss Dens insisted that she stay. "This is far more important than anything else she could be doing."

She turned to Squint and said, "I suppose you want me to tell you all about my myself."

Squint's usual method with new customers *was* to talk to them and get a feel for their issues. However, Squint got the impression she would be here forever if she used that approach with Miss Dens. She decided to get right to the point.

"First, I'll need to touch you to get an idea of how I can help you," she said.

While she was in Norla, one of her clients had commented on her skill at using healing talents, Squint had realized that she should be more careful about displaying her talents., so she had immediately began working on hiding her healing talents She had became quite adept at using herbs and other healing methods to mask her talents.

Since Miss Dens refused to leave the bed, she reluctantly allowed Squint to sit next to her. Squint took the young lady's hand and closed her eyes. After a thorough "examination," Squint determined that there was nothing physically wrong with Miss Dens.

"This will be much easier if we move to the table, where we can have some tea while we continue," she said.

With a great many dramatic sighs, Miss Dens arose from her bed to sit at the small table with Squint.

Once they were comfortably settled, Squint asked Miss Dens to explain what her symptoms were.

And, as she had suspected, it took forever. It was nearing lunch time when Squint finally called a halt to the young lady's litany of complaints.

"I think I know what needs to be done," she said.

She turned to Jenda and said, "Will you bring us some hot water, and then leave us, please? I'd like to talk to Miss Dens alone."

Once Jenda brought the hot water and retreated, Squint said, "I think I have just what you need. But you must understand that the things I'm giving you are very rare indeed."

Squint reached into the left pocket of her skirt and withdrew two small vials, one blue and one green.

"I'll need a clean teacup, please," she said. Miss Dens quickly handed Squint a cup from the tea service that was sitting on the table between them.

Squint raised the blue vial. "This vial contains water from the deepest region of the Byfay River", she said solemnly. "Please be still. I must be very careful in my measurements."

Squint carefully tipped the vial over the teacup. "One drop, exactly one drop, is what we need."

She returned the blue vial to her pocket. Now she raised the green vial.

"This vial contains sand from the lowest regions of the Dahine Desert." She pulled some tiny pincers from her pocket. "One grain. No more, and no less." She used the pincers and placed one grain of sand in the cup.

"Now for the most important ingredient," she said. "I just got a new shipment of this yesterday." She reached into her right pocket and removed her pocket towel. She unfolded the towel to reveal four small dark pink petals.

"These petals come from the rarest of all plants, the Gainsly Rose. They grow only in the darkest regions of the Gainsly Forest. They bloom for only one night, once every ten years, and the bloom is only fully open for a few moments. The petals must be plucked during that short time."

She placed one of the petals in the cup. "Now we need exactly three drops of hot water." She carefully poured three drops of hot water into the teacup.

"Now we must wait exactly three minutes."

After three minutes, she solemnly handed Miss Dens the cup. "Drink it quickly now."

Miss Dens tipped the cup and quickly drank the "potion".

"You should start feeling better immediately," Squint said. "Now that you've taken the potion, there are some things you'll need to do to make sure the effects are permanent."

These things, not the potion, were what Lialey Dens really needed. "You will need fresh air daily. I suggest that you spend some time at the park each day. Perhaps you could take lunch with you, and some bread crumbs to feed the birds."

After a bit of thought, she said, "You will also need something with which you can occupy your time. My friend Twell holds art classes each week. He has an exclusive clientele, but I believe he will be happy to include you."

She reached across the table and took Miss Dens' hands in hers. Looking her in the eyes, she said, "It is very important for your health that you do these things Miss Dens. I fear what will happen if you do not."

Letting go of Miss Dens' hands, she said, "If you like, I can come back and take you to your first art class."

And with everything settled, she was finally able to leave.

She headed for the park where she usually ate lunch. She needed a few minutes to unwind before she headed for her next appointment.

She headed for her usual bench near the lake, in the center of the park. When she got close, she noticed a man was there, reading a book. He looked familiar, although she was sure if she had met him before, she would remember. He was very handsome.

She decided to introduce herself, and continued toward the bench. Just before she reached the bench, she heard quiet sniffling off to her left. Turning, she saw a very young girl, sitting in the grass with her head in her hands. With one more glance at the handsome man, she turned and went to the little girl.

She sat down beside the girl and said, "Hi, my name is Serran, what's yours?"

"My name is Mouli, but everybody calls me Mouse."

"Do you have a pocket towel, Mouse?" asked Squint.

"No, I forgot."

Squint dug out her pocket towel and handed it to the little girl. "Well, Mouse, why is it you're so sad?"

After she wiped her nose with the pocket towel, Mouli said, "Me and my brother are s'posed to wait for Mama in the park, but he went off to play with his friends. He wouldn't let me go with him. Now I got nobody to play with."

"I'd be happy to keep you company until your mama or brother gets back, if you like," said Squint."

'Okay, but will you call me Mouli. I hate being called Mouse."

"Why," asked Squint, "don't you like mice?"

"No. They're little."

"Yes, they are," said Squint, "but they're also quick, and they're smart."

Mouli looked at her and said, "Smart?"

"Sure. They must be smart to stay out of people's traps, right?"

At this point, Squint noticed that the man on the bench had stopped reading, and was listening to the conversation.

Mouli thought for a moment, and said, "Yeah."

"Besides," said Squint, "they're really cute."

"At least your family calls you Mouse. Mine called me Squint." Squint heard the man's book drop, and glanced at him.

"Squint, that's a silly name. Why would they call you that?"

"Well," said Squint, "when I was little, my father used to say that I was so small he had to squint to see me. Pretty soon, everyone was calling me Squint, and it stuck."

She looked to see what the man thought of that, but he was gone.

Disappointed, she turned back to Mouli, and said, "But you know what? I like it. It's a special name, just for me. It makes me feel special."

Mouli thought about this for a bit. "You know what, I think I like being called Mouse. It's my special name."

Squint stayed with Mouli until her brother returned. When he realized how upset his sister was at being left alone, he felt terrible, and promised her he would never leave her by herself again.

Looking at his face, Squint believed he meant it.

As she left the park and headed for her next appointment, Squint was thinking about the handsome man. It was strange. She felt like she knew him from somewhere, but was equally sure that, as handsome as he was, if she had met him, she would remember.

A few days later, Squint returned to take Miss Dens to her art classes. Jenda answered her knock at the door. Much to Squint's surprise, Miss Dens was ready to go.

"Let's get this over with," she said, and marched out the door. They made the entire trip to Twell's art gallery in silence. After introducing Miss Dens and leaving her in Twell's good hands, Squint left, wondering how long the arrangement would last.

Several weeks later, Squint found herself with some extra time, so she decided to stop and see how Miss Dens was doing. Unlike her last visit, she was greeted at the door by Miss Dens herself. She was smiling, and when Squint greeted her as Miss Dens, she said, "Oh, call me Lialey. I'm so glad to see you."

She escorted Squint to the day room. She asked Squint to sit, and said, "Let me just go ask Jenda if she'll make some tea and join us."

"Jenda," thought Squint. It was the first time she had heard Lialey refer to her as anything other than "the housewoman". This was certainly an improvement. And inviting her to join them was another first.

By the end of the visit, it was clear that her "potion" and the following "treatment" had a profound effect on the young woman. She talked about herself, but included both Squint and Jenda in the conversation. And she no longer talked about her ailments. She appeared to be a happy, normal young woman.

Once again, it was much later than her usual lunchtime when she left the house. But it was certainly under much better circumstances. She had no afternoon commitments, so she decided to go to the park for a bit, and then go see what she could do for Miss Aagne.

As she neared "her" bench, she spotted the same handsome man she had seen last time she visited Lialey Dens. He was, once again, reading a book. This time, she made it to the bench without incident.

"Hello," she said. "May I sit here?"

The man jumped, and nearly dropped his book. He looked up at Squint, and then looked like he wanted to get up and run.

He gestured at the bench with his book, and Squint sat down.

"My name is Serran," she said.

Still looking like he wanted to get up and run, he replied "My name is Quellan."

Now it was her turn to jump. "Quellan? Quellan Greves?"

"No wonder I felt I knew him," she thought.

"Yes, I'm Quellan Greves. Do I know you?"

"Well, sort of." she replied. "I'm also known as Squint."

He just stared at her. "Squint's a boy," he finally said.

"It's a long story. Look, let's get this out of the way right now. I do not blame you for what happened in Kenna. It was as much my fault as yours. Maybe more."

Quellan continued to stare at her. "That doesn't make any more sense than Squint turning into a girl."

"I guess I should explain."

Squint talked for several hours. She explained about her talents, and about how she was just starting to learn about them at the time of the incident. She explained how the fireballs he had thrown at her had been deflected by a talent that she hadn't even known she had.

She also explained that, although she had seen Quellan, no one else had. She said that she had seen the look on his face, and knew that he had not meant to hurt anyone. She also told him about her reasons for pretending to be a boy. That it has started out as a way to attend the academy. And that once she learned about the Magician, it became a necessity.

She was not sure why she trusted Quellan with all this information, but she somehow knew it was safe.

When she was done, Quellan talked about his life since he left the academy. He said that he had been totally horrified by what he had done. He had started running, and for several months, he had just kept running. Trying to get away from his own feelings, he supposed. When he had finally stopped running and taken stock of things, he was close to Greyn, and had decided to stay a while. Afraid someone would be looking for him, he chose a new name, and started a new life. He wandered from town to town, unable to settle anywhere.

He ended up in Echan about three years ago. When he arrived, he decided he was done looking over his shoulder. He'd go back to using his real name, and take his punishment when they caught up with him.

They also talked about Quellan's treatment of Squint at the academy. He said that, in the beginning, he envied the ease with which Squint learned, while he had to work so hard at it. It annoyed him that Squint clearly did not care about how well he did on tests, when it was all Quellan could think about.

As time went by, and he had to work harder and harder to do well, he got more and more angry at how easy things were for Squint. It got to where he just couldn't stand the sight of him. Even though he knew it was not right, he began picking on the small boy. He didn't know when things go so out of hand that he was actually trying to hurt Squint.

It was almost dark when they finished talking. They were both emotionally exhausted, but neither wanted to end the meeting. They decided to meet again the next day.

After that, they met at the park several times a week. Eventually, Quellan told her about a spot he had found not far south of town that would be a perfect picnic spot.

It was a meadow about three hours to the south of town. It was at the bottom of a large dip in the land, and it really was a perfect spot for picnics. On one of their visits, Squint said that the dip looked like a giant had pressed his thumb into the world, and the two of them started calling the meadow the Thumb Print. The two began to meet more and more often. The bench by the lake in the park and the Thumb Print were their favorite spots.

Squint told Quellan about Vayan and Beldon, and she talked about them often. About six months after their first meeting at the park, Squint took Quellan to meet them. Although neither man knew of Quellan's involvement in the incident with Young Donald, both knew how he had hounded Squint at the academy.

Squint said that she knew Quellan was a big bully, but that the birds at the park liked him, so she supposed she could forgive him. Thankfully, it didn't take long before both men came to like Quellan, and were happy to have him join Squint on her visits.

One year after their first meeting, Squint and Quellan were married. They held the linking at Vayan's house in Belt. Since neither she nor Quellan had family, the only witnesses to the linking were

Vayan, his wife Joyen, and Beldon. Although small, it was a beautiful ceremony, and Joyen made a huge feast for afterwards.

CHAPTER 24

On Sunday morning, the first day of midden, Quellan found Squint in the kitchen, packing food into a picnic basket. She must have been up for some time, because she had not only prepared whatever was in the basket, but had already tidied the kitchen.

She smiled at him and said, "It looks like it's going to be a beautiful day, so I thought we could have a picnic at The Thumb Print today."

As he reached around her for the basket lid, he asked, "What did you pack?"

She smacked his hand, and said, "You can find out at lunch time. If you weren't so lazy, you could have helped me, instead of sleeping the day away. Then you would know what's in here."

She had some wonderful news for Quellan, and wanted things to be perfect when she shared it with him. She had fixed his favorite picnic lunch, and had included a bottle of wine to celebrate with.

Squint was right, it was turning out to be a lovely day. They took their time walking, enjoying the weather and being with each other with nothing to do. They reached the meadow mid-morning, and were looking for the perfect spot for their picnic, when there was a huge boom, and Quellan fell at Squint's feet.

She dropped down beside him, and knew instantly that he was dead. She looked around frantically, trying to find something that would explain what had just happened.

To the west, at the edge of the dip leading into the meadow, she could see the outline of a man. Without knowing how she knew, since he was too far away for her to make out any details, she knew that this was the Magician, and that the final confrontation was here.

She had no time to grieve, as she was instantly bombarded with a massive burst of energy.

And so it began.

It was dusk, and Squint was crouching quietly behind a small outcropping of rocks. She had no idea how long they'd been at this, but it seemed like forever. They had been bouncing magic off each other's shields, and accomplishing nothing. She had to try something else. As she rose to move, she slid slightly on some loose pebbles. This gave her an idea.

She lowered her defenses just enough to heighten her sight. She needed to know precisely where the Magician was.

There.

Taking a deep breath, she froze the ground underneath him, and then immediately flung shards of ice at him. She aimed the shards low, hoping the ice on the ground would catch him off guard and he would be falling by the time the shards reached him.

IT WORKED!

She heard him grunt as he slid on the ice, and then he went down. She had managed to time the shards of ice perfectly, and he was hit hard on his way down.

Not waiting to see any more, she immediately traveled to a new place, and slammed her shields back in place. Hopefully she was able to do some real damage this time.

Tired.

She was running out of energy. Once again, she burrowed into the ground and curled up to rest. She couldn't understand how the Magician kept going. As far as she could tell, he wasn't resting at all, and yet he seemed to have plenty of energy.

After a short time, she made her way out of the little cave she had created and searched for the Magician. Before she found him, she heard him cry out in pain.

She was having trouble locating him. She heightened her sight, and finally found him. No wonder she'd had trouble locating him. He was almost sitting on the ground. It looked like he had one leg stuck in a hole.

When she realized what must have happened, she almost laughed. It appeared that he had found one of her resting places.

She took the opportunity to bombard him with magic. She was sure she had hit him several times before he was able to extricate himself from the hole and disappear.

She was exhausted.

Squint had no idea how much time had passed since Quellan's death, but she could not go on. With her last bit of energy, she created a small cave, and crawled in. Once again, she curled up to rest. As she always did in times of need, she reached up to grasp her birthday necklace.

As she closed her hand around the stone, she felt her energy return. It was not a gradual return. It was instant and complete. She was no longer exhausted. Her muscles were still sore, her many wounds still hurt, but she no longer felt drained.

And something else happened. Without knowing how or why she knew this, she knew the stone was her salvation. She knew that, as long as she had the stone, she could not die at the hands of the Magician. This was why the stone was special. This was why it had been passed down through the years.

The legends had it wrong. She wasn't the Receptacle, the stone was. She was simply the keeper of the stone. It had imbued her with the power to keep it safe until it was time to fight the Magician.

She reached up and unclasped the chain from her neck. She removed the stone from the chain. Holding the stone tightly in her hand, she crawled out of the cave she had created.

She stood straight and looked around. She didn't see the Magician, but she knew he was still there. She found Quellan's body a short distance away, and moved toward it. She sat down beside him and crossed her legs. She put her hands in her lap, gently cradled the Receptacle, and waited.

She didn't have to wait long.

The Magician appeared over the rise directly in front of her. He paused, as if trying to figure out what she was up to. She just sat.

And once again, it started.

He bombarded her with magic. Again. And again. And each time, the stone appeared to absorb the magic. She did nothing. She simply sat there, calmly letting the stone take care of things.

This apparently infuriated the Magician. With more and more anger, he threw magic after magic in her direction, only to have it disappear in her hands.

"NO," he shouted.

"I

WILL

NOT

LET

YOU

WIN."

As if to emphasize his statement, with each word, he threw another, greater magic.

Finally, he stood, hands raised, gathering his power.

"YOU **WILL** DIE!" he screamed, and flung a massive ball of pure energy at her.

This time, the stone did not absorb the energy, it deflected it. Directly back to the Magician.

There was a brief scream, and he was gone.

The stone went cold in her hand, and with that, she knew it was over.

CHAPTER 25

Joyen was at the sink washing dishes when she heard a noise behind her. She turned to find Squint, leaning heavily on the table. She was dirty, with cuts and bruises everywhere, and was quite obviously exhausted.

"It's over, Joyen. Tell him it's over. Tell him I'm sorry. I have to go. Please, tell him I'm sorry."

And she was gone just as quickly as she'd arrived.

Beldon was sitting at his desk, fiddling with some papers when Squint appeared before him. She nearly fell over, and grabbed the edge of his desk for support.

"It's done, Beldon. It's done. I'm sorry. I'm so sorry. I can't stay. I need to rest. I'm sorry."

And with that, she was gone.

After she visited her two friends to tell them it was over, Squint went home. Not to Echan, where she lived with Quellan. She couldn't face that yet. She traveled to her home outside Kenna, and without even bothering to clean up, collapsed on her bed.

She had no idea how long she slept, but when she woke, she was hungry. As she headed to the kitchen, she realized that she was still exhausted, and that she was dirtier than she could ever remember being. She detoured to the bathroom, and cleaned up. She tended to her wounds the best she could, and headed back to the kitchen.

And realized there would be no food there. She didn't want to go to the house she had shared with Quellan, but she needed food.

After taking care of her hunger, sleeping for a while longer, and once again tending to her wounds, there were two things she needed to do. She needed to go back to The Thumb Print and lay Quellan to rest. And she had to tell Vayan and Beldon what had happened.

After a brief, painful day of flames ceremony for Quellan, Squint set out to talk to her friends. She traveled to Melsta first, and found Beldon at his desk. She greeted him with a hug, and asked, "Do you have time to travel with me to Belt to see Vayan? I need to talk to you both, and I'd rather not have to explain things twice."

Beldon rushed around the desk and pulled Squint into his arms. With obvious concern, he looked down at her and said, "What happened to you. I've been worried sick. Are you okay? You look like you're half dead."

"Let's go find Vayan," she replied.

This time, she took them to Vayan's shop. Last time, she had been so exhausted, the Wakes' kitchen was the only place she could remember well enough to travel to safely.

When they arrived in the furniture shop, Vayan rushed over to Squint, pulled her into a bear hug, and almost word for word, repeated Beldon's greeting.

After assuring them that she would survive, Squint suggested they go somewhere comfortable, since her explanation would take a while.

They walked from the furniture shop to the Wakes home, and after greeting Joyen, settled down on the porch.

"When I stopped by here two days ago," Squint began, and was instantly interrupted by both men.

"Squint, that was five days ago, not two," said Beldon.

She stared at them for a moment, and then said, "What day is it today?"

"It's the ninth of midden."

She looked at them both, and said "So I was last here on the fourth? I spent nearly four full days in battle?"

After a thoughtful pause, she shrugged and went back to her tale.

It was dusk by the time she finished the telling.

"I know you must be angry that I didn't come for you, but I just didn't have time," she said.

"Squint, we're both glad that you're here, safe and sound, and the Magician is dead. Nothing else matters," said Vayan. "And considering what happened to Quellan, it's probably best that we weren't there."

Beldon nodded in agreement.

Joyen came to the door and asked if they were done talking. "I don't want to interrupt, but I really think Squint needs to eat something."

With a smile at Joyen, Squint said, "If it's your cooking, then I am in desperate need of food."

After dinner, while Joyen cleared the table, Beldon said, "Squint, this might not be the right time for this, but what was the news you had for Quellan that day?"

And for the first time since Quellan's death, Squint wept.

When she finally got her emotions under control, she told them that she was going to have a baby.

"If I had just told him about it, and not decided to make such a big deal out of it, he would still be here," she said.

"That's just not true, Squint," said Vayan. "Think about it. You and Quellan spent most of your time together. It's almost certain that the Magician would have found you two together wherever he encountered you. And, just as he did, he would have killed Quellan, either to get him out of the way, or in the hopes of upsetting you enough to weaken you."

"You know he's right," agreed Beldon. "You can't take the blame for the Magician's hatred. The battle was predestined, and the Magician was determined to destroy you, Quellan, and everyone else."

Joyen stood next to Squint, and put a hand on her shoulder. She said, "Squint, you must stay here with us. We can take care of you and the baby, and you'll have nothing to worry about."

Squint rose and hugged Joyen. "As much as I would love that, I need to get on with my life. I have to decide what I want to do now."

She got up and gave each of them a hug. "I've spent my entire life preparing for an encounter with the Magician. Right now, I feel like I have no purpose. I need to decide what to do next."

She stood in thought for a moment, and said," For now, I'm going to go back to Echan to clear things up. I know I don't want to live there without Quellan. After that, I'm not sure what I'm going to do, but I do know I need to get on with my life, and I won't be able to do that if I stay here."

CHAPTER 26

Serran, as she was now known, spent the next two months clearing up business in Echan. She spent a good deal of her time resting and getting her health back. While she went about her business, she had plenty of time to think about what she wanted to do with her life.

Of all the places she had traveled, she had been happiest and felt most at home in Ander. She decided she would like to go back there and find out if Serran could be as good a friend to Marmie as Squint had. There would be no need to hide her talents, and she would have ample opportunities to make a living.

Once she had made the decision, she was quick to act on it. With short stops in Melsta and Belt to visit her friends and let them know of her decision, Serran traveled to the same spot just north of Ander where Squint had brought Vayan and Beldon, so long ago.

In Ander, she went directly to Terr Fost's book stand. Introducing herself as Serran Nylls, she explained that she was a widow looking for a new start. She said that she and her husband had traveled through Ander some time ago, and she had liked it so much she wanted to settle here. She asked if he might know of a place to stay while she arranged things.

Once again, Mr. Fost took her to Mrs. Gern's home and introduced her. Mrs. Gern looked at Serran and said, "Do I know you, young woman? You seem very familiar to me."

With a pang of guilt for lying, Serran said, "No, I don't believe we've met before."

In no time at all, Serran had settled in to her new life. She found a small house near the center of town. It would be just big enough for her and the baby. Once again, she provided healing services free of charge. However, rather than odd jobs, she settled on a new profession that allowed her to work from her home. She put to use her talent as a seamstress, and made traveling cloaks for both men and women.

She and Marmie quickly became the best of friends. She frequently helped Marmie at the book stand, and just as frequently, Marmie helped Serran with her sewing.

She and Marmie talked about everything, including Serran's traveling talent. She had explained it to Marmie, because once a week or so, she would travel to Melsta and Belt to visit with Vayan and Beldon. Serran spoke often of her two friends, but was careful not to use their names. She wasn't sure if Marmie would remember them, but she didn't want to find out. She was afraid of losing Marmie's friendship. It was her last secret, and she hated it, but she didn't know what else to do.

As her birth time came near, her visits to her two friends became less frequent. She was concerned about how traveling might affect the baby. And besides, she was getting as big as a house, and preferred to stay home, where she was comfortable.

When Serran's birth time came, Marmie brought the local mother's assistant to help with the birth. Marmie stayed right beside Serran, and held her hand. As the three soon discovered, it was no wonder Serran had gotten so big. She wasn't having *a* baby, she was having *two*!

Serran had a boy and a girl, and named them Quellan and Cayrah. They were in good health, and were both very happy babies.

When they were about a month old, she asked Marmie if she would watch them for a short while, so she could visit her friends and share the good news. After that, Marmie would watch the children for a short time each week while Serran traveled to either Belt or Melsta.

Serran and her children settled into a comfortable routine. Quellan was a quiet, studious child, much like Serran had been, while Cayrah was much more like her father. They were both curious, and quick to learn.

The week before their third birthday, Serran visited both Vayan and Beldon, and asked if they would be willing to have a small birthday party for the two children. She said she and the children would travel to Melsta and gather Beldon, and then they could all spend the day at Vayan's.

She left gifts for both of them with Vayan, and left Joyen making elaborate plans for a birthday party.

She should have known it wouldn't be a small party. But it was a great success. Vayan and Beldon seemed to have a contest going to see who could spoil the children the most, with Joyen right behind.

One of the gifts from Serran to Cayrah was a small stone, beautifully set in silver filigree, hung on a slender silver chain. The stone itself was more or less oval in shape, about the size of a large grape. It was translucent, with tiny streaks of color that changed with the light. The colors no longer changed with Serran's mood. She knew that it was now nothing more than a lovely stone, but she wanted Cayrah to have it.

When they got home that evening, Marmie was waiting to hear all the details.

Cayrah jumped in Marmie's lap and, with a huge grin on her face, said, "You know what? Uncle Beldon and Aunt Joyen and Uncle Vayan call mother Squint. Isn't that funny?"

Squint was stunned, and she looked at Marmie to see how she reacted. What she saw shocked her even more.

Marmie took one look at Squint's face, and burst out laughing. Both Quellan and Cayrah looked confused by her laughter.

"It wasn't that funny, Aunt Marmie," said Quellan, with a puzzled look on his face.

"Oh, Serran," said Marmie. "You have absolutely no idea how amazing that is." She grinned hugely at Serran, and said, "Ever since you moved here, you've reminded me of Squint. There were so many things that you did and said that reminded me of him. Next to you, he was the best friend I ever had, and when he left, I never stopped missing him. Now I know why you remind me so much of him."

"Marmie, you're the best friend I've ever had. When I first moved here, I wanted nothing more than to start a new life. As myself. And then I couldn't figure out how to tell you that I was Squint. Now and again, you would talk about Squint, but I was afraid that, if I told you I was Squint, you would hate me for lying to you."

Marmie went to Serran and wrapped her in her arms. "Oh, Serran," she said, "Nothing you do will make me hate you. You're my best friend. But some day you're going to have to tell me why you were masquerading as a boy. And how you managed to look and sound so much like a boy."

And with that, Serran gave up her last secret, and finally put Squint to rest.

Printed in Great Britain
by Amazon

43692988R00109